Penguin Crime Fiction
The Detective Wore Silk Drawers

Peter Lovesey, born in Whitton, Middlesex, in 1936,
attended Hampton Grammar School and Reading
University and was a Head of Department at Hammersmith
and West London College until 1975, when he became a
professional author. His crime-writing career began with
Wobble to Death, a Victorian detective story which won the
Macmillan/Panther First Crime Novel Award in 1970. The
series of novels featuring Detective Sergeant Cribb reflects
his strong interest in the Victorian social and sporting
scenes. His other novels include *Invitation to a Dynamite
Party*, *A Case of Spirits*, *Swing, Swing Together* and
Waxwork, which won the Crime Writers' Association
Silver Dagger Award for 1978.

Peter Lovesey met his wife at university; they live in
Surrey with their son and daughter.

Peter Lovesey

The Detective
Wore Silk Drawers

Penguin Books

Penguin Books Ltd, Harmondsworth,
Middlesex, England
Penguin Books, 625 Madison Avenue,
New York, New York 10022, U.S.A.
Penguin Books Australia Ltd, Ringwood,
Victoria, Australia
Penguin Books Canada Ltd, 2801 John Street,
Markham, Ontario, Canada L3R 1B4
Penguin Books (N.Z.) Ltd, 182-190 Wairau Road,
Auckland 10, New Zealand

First published in Great Britain by Macmillan London Ltd 1971
First published in the United States of America
by Dodd, Mead & Company 1971
Published in Penguin Books 1980

Made and printed in Great Britain by
Richard Clay (The Chaucer Press), Ltd,
Bungay, Suffolk
Set in Plantin

One

Sergeant Cribb sat with his pint of Bass East India, moodily watching the froth disperse. A glass at the Ratcatcher, supped in solitude after work, was his usual antidote for a hard day. Murder or arson, rape or robbery, he would seldom allow duty to break the routine. At the bar he was recognized as a regular. The ale was drawn for him between entry, bowing under a low beam and arrival at the counter. He would then produce twopence, nod to Ada and look about for an empty table. For twenty minutes or more he was anonymous. The station knew where he was all right – poor bobbies they'd have been if they hadn't – but heaven help the orderly who disturbed him now.

'Punch cartoon coppers.' That was typical of Jowett. A calculated insult, delivered with a curl of the lip, and no doubt who was meant. Sitting there under his halo of pipe-smoke, pontificating about the new style of detective. Cribb had known this would happen as soon as rumours began to emanate from the Yard about the new Director's ideas. If one thing was predictable in these uncertain times it was that Inspector Jowett would embrace the current orthodoxy.

Cribb, meanwhile, had stood to attention in the carpeted office, appearing to listen. What was Jowett? A sandwich-man without boards, with a new message each time you met him. He was one of the few at the Yard who emerged unscathed from the Turf Fraud Scandal of 1877, when the Detective Department's three Chief-Inspectors stood in the dock at the Old Bailey accused of conspiracy, and two were convicted. Heads had rolled in plenty after that. Not Jowett's though. Who knew what he stood for?

Cribb lifted the glass and drank deeply. The whole episode

was unexpected. It had started as a perfectly straightforward Monday: cab to the station, letters to sort, the Duke Street assault and battery to write up, a pleasantly dull morning. Then the call from the Yard. What could Jowett want with him? There the Inspector sat among unread books and leather-bound furniture drawing at that infernal briar between the well-prepared insults. 'Bow Street methods.' Nothing, of course, in personal terms. 'Jumped-up beat pounders.' Superficially the approach was affable: 'Not long since we were sergeants together, eh?' The talk was all of backward-looking colleagues who would not survive long in the new C.I.D.

Cribb, like the rest, well remembered the notice:

Criminal Investigation Department
From Monday next, April 8th, the whole of the detective establishment will form one body under the Director of Criminal Investigation. With the exception of the undermentioned officers, promoted or appointed to responsible posts, the present staff will be placed on probation for three months ...

It was galling to read the names that followed, comprehending that yours did not appear. And the next three months had been harder still, as rumours circulated of new purges. But that was all two years ago, and Cribb now had two or three successful murder investigations to his credit. When the call came from Jowett, even the thought of promotion had crossed his mind.

'D'you understand French at all, Sergeant?'

'No, sir.'

'Pity, that. Great pity. The Director is quite a linguist. Made a study of the Paris *Sûreté*. Brilliant.'

'So we've been told, sir.'

Jowett didn't like that.

'Mr Vincent may be young, Sergeant, but he's fly enough to have impressed the Home Secretary. Don't under-estimate him.'

While the Inspector expanded on the need to be responsive to new leadership, Cribb speculated on the purpose of this interview. Promotion was already out of the question. Dismissal? He

6

doubted that. Not after a special commendation for the Islington cases. His record since Vincent took over was unspotted.

'To come to the point, Sergeant, we need to re-examine our methods. How efficient are they? Don't try to answer – I'm putting points. When a crime is perpetrated how quickly do we act? How much are we hampered by the elaborateness of our organization? You see the line of reasoning? Fresh methods, new approaches. The man we need in Criminal Investigation is the man with flair – never mind the long records of selfless service, Cribb. Devotion doesn't count for much in your French detective department.'

So this was the newest Jowett affectation. Cribb had often thought Scotland Yard cumbersome, but what the French could teach them he did not know.

'Take a case that nobody can crack,' went on the Inspector. 'You know the drill – months of inquiries, plenty of suspicions, but nothing affirmative. Your English detective admits he's beaten and puts the whole lot away in a drawer marked "unsolved". Now what does the *Sûreté* do in a similar predicament? Probably you wouldn't know the term –'

Cribb had borne enough. '*Agent Provocateur?*' he suggested in a passable accent.

In his corner of the bar he smiled faintly at the recollection. It had so jolted Jowett that for a second he had forgotten his theme and taken to compulsively refilling his pipe. Then the monologue had restarted in earnest, the jabbing phrases increasing in frequency as he reasserted himself. In an effort to suppress his impatience Cribb had concentrated on trying to read the book titles behind Jowett.

'Wouldn't work here, of course. The law doesn't allow it. Conspiracy to commit a crime. No need to remind you of that, eh? But a spry detective finds ways of getting to the truth, Sergeant. Your French investigator uses this' – and Jowett tapped his forehead. 'Over the Channel they're not so narrow in their thinking as some of our bobbies. A hansom always has the beating of a tram because it doesn't run on rails, you see.' Pleased with this analogy, he unexpectedly invited Cribb to sit down.

'Less formality, Sergeant. That is the key to greater efficiency in this Department. Inspiration, intuition and flair! How many undetected outbreaks of crime have you recorded in your Division?'

'This year, sir?'

'Naturally.'

'Major crimes, sir?'

'Of course.'

'Must be forty or more.'

Jowett leaned forward. 'Forty-seven, in fact, since New Year's Day. I checked the figure. Far too many. How do you propose to reduce the number?'

Cribb tried to sound convincing. 'Patient inquiries, sir. We investigate every possibility. When there's a development, we're poised ready to act.'

Jowett's eyebrows lifted at the centre in a drawbridge motion. 'Awaiting developments, eh? Sitting in the station poised over a pot of tea? Don't look alarmed, Sergeant. I'm not criticizing you in particular. You and I know what it is like to work at a case for days and be left with nothing of substance. And don't think me unappreciative of what the Waterloo area is like. We gave you one of the seedy patches, Cribb, and that we recognize.' His smile suggested nothing so generous. 'But forty-seven! Now that wants looking into, wouldn't you say?'

What could he say?

'I'm looking at you, Sergeant – and others, superior to me, are looking – for a swift reduction in that number. Take my advice and re-examine your methods of investigation. We're in the Eighties now.' He eyed the new telephone-set on his desk. 'Science is taking over. And naturally I want to help in any way that I am able. Do you have the staff that you need?'

'Yes, sir. Capable men. But there is one detective constable attached to S Division I used to work with –'

'Who's that?'

'Constable Thackeray, sir. Not a young man. He knew my ways better than most.'

'You shall have him.'

'Thank you, sir.'

'That's all, then, Sergeant. We shall watch for developments in your Division.'

'Very good, sir.'

Poor Thackeray. A posting to Cribb's Division would not please him much. For eight months since his last case with Cribb he had worked conscientiously in S Division (Hampstead was not noted for its crime-rate) scoring enough small successes to justify promotion to sergeant before his retirement.

Cribb upended his tankard. Then he withdrew a handkerchief to wipe the corners of his mouth. The bar-parlour was less crowded than usual. Ada at the counter was flirting with one of her regulars, a stocky pawnbroker whose professional indiscretions were unforgivable if his endless patter could be believed. At the end of the room a group of navvies clustered around a bagatelle board, and to their left a pair of shabby professional men – solicitors' clerks perhaps – hungrily bolted thickly sliced bread. Bread and cheese always sold well here, day and evening. A plateful of heart-shaped cakes, topped with cherries, under a glass dome on the counter, never seemed to sell, except when customers took them to their children waiting outside.

'Jumped-up beat-pounders.' Cribb grunted audibly at the memory and thrust the handkerchief deep into his trouser-pocket. There were sixteen Divisions in the Metropolitan area, excluding A Division, which was Central Office. Fourteen of them were headed by inspectors. Two sergeants with Divisional responsibility, and he had to be one.

An engraving of a bull-terrier hung over the piano to Cribb's left, an ugly, bow-legged brute, mainly yellow, but once white, with a smear of black across the haunches. On Saturdays and Bank Holidays singers would group around the piano, facing old Patch as they chorused by the hour. Few ever read the small print beneath: *'Mr Howard Shore's champion dog, Leamington, which caught and killed 302 rats in one hour at the Hare and Billet, Wimbledon, 7th May 1863'*. The sergeant scanned Leamington, and pondered his secret. Inspiration, intuition or flair?

Science, anyway, had never bothered him. Cribb stood up to leave.

'Mr Cribb, sir. Can you spare a moment? This gentleman wants a word with you?'

The sergeant did not like his name bandied in public. He had not realized before that Ada knew it. Barmaids are intuitive detectives.

It was not the pawnbroker who had asked for Cribb but an old man, lean and nearly toothless, wrapped in an ill-fitting overcoat. It smelt of fish.

Cribb asked what he wanted.

'It's worth a drink, mister.'

'It had better be. Two more pints, Ada.'

He carried the drinks back to his table, with the old man shuffling behind. Both took a long drink before anything was spoken.

'What's your business, then?' Cribb asked sceptically.

Bloodshot eyes studied him as the old man took his drink.

'You're a blue, ain't you, mister? You don't wear the jacket but you're one of 'em, ain't you?'

The sergeant confirmed that he was.

'Well then, bobby. What's a corpse worth to you?'

'Depends,' answered Cribb. 'What's the game? If it's bodies you're trading in, then you won't want the police.'

'One body, that's all. I found it.'

'Where?'

'Five bob.'

'Man or woman?'

'Man, if I ain't mistaken. Not ten minutes from 'ere.'

Cribb, who had met casual informants before, drew out his watch. 'Sorry. Must be going now. We'll find your corpse if it's that near.'

'Four bob, then,' suggested the old man.

Cribb walked to the bar and returned his tankard. The informant left his drink to intercept the sergeant as he made for the door.

'Three bob?' he pleaded.

Cribb looked down witheringly. 'Three bob for what? It don't need a sharp nose to tell me you deal in cockles and whelks, and the only stalls I know here-abouts are in Stamford Street, near Blackfriars Bridge. And I've worked long enough in these parts to have fished a few drowned corpses out of the mud along there. They jump off Waterloo Bridge at the rate of three or four a month. It's got a powerful attraction for desperate men that can't swim a stroke. No, old friend. One body washed down-stream to Blackfriars doesn't excite me overmuch. Now will you let me pass?'

The swift deductions silenced the old man, but he followed Cribb into the street, trying to re-engage his attention as he looked about for a cab.

'What if it was a murdered corpse, bobby?'

Cribb ignored him.

'You can't by-pass a murder.'

A cab was approaching.

' 'E were murdered, bobby.'

Cribb relented. 'How do you know?'

The informant cackled.

' 'Cause 'eadless corpses don't jump off bridges.'

'Headless?'

'From the neck upwards, bobby.'

'This had better be true.' Cribb drew a half-crown from his pocket. 'Get in the cab, then.'

'Barge 'Ouse Street,' the old man shouted to the cabman. 'You know it? Off Upper Ground.'

' 'Ere, just a moment, guv. Can't take the likes of 'im. Got my other passengers to think of!' The cabby lifted his whip to move off.

Cribb snapped his fingers. 'Police. No co-operation: no licence. Follow me?'

The cabby grumbled copiously to himself as they climbed inside, Cribb taking a deep breath of fresh air before joining his fellow-passenger. It would not be too long. Best, in the circumstances, to put his mind on more important matters. He thought of Jowett.

'Forty-eight,' he said to himself glumly.

Two

Cribb's guide led at a step brisk enough to be almost unseemly for one so elderly. They cut behind the few derelict buildings that fringed on the no man's land of the river-edge. Their arrival had already caused a stir in the neighbourhood. A hansom in Barge House Street was as rare as a porpoise upriver. Once it was established that the visitor was neither magistrate nor schoolmaster a small train of curious boys hitched on to Cribb, with three or four muttering women at a discreet distance behind.

The object of their visit lay as the tide had deposited it, toes upwards in a small irregularity in the bank. Cribb turned abruptly on the children and ordered them back to the houses.

'You found this yourself?' he asked the old man.

'Yes. Not two hours back. Tide must have washed 'im up.'

'You didn't touch him?'

'Nah. I wouldn't do that. What'd I want to do that for? If 'e 'ad any money on 'im I reckon the cove what lopped 'is head off 'ad that.'

Cribb admitted the shrewdness of this with a nod. Even so, he bent to turn out the sodden pockets. All were empty.

'Big fellow, I reckon,' observed the old man. 'Take more than one to fell 'im, if you ask me.'

'Strong physique,' admitted Cribb, unbuttoning the shirt to look for tattooing. 'No great height, though, even when he was complete. Five-eight, I'd say.'

'The 'ead shouldn't be difficult to match up when you find it. There's a good ginger thatch on 'is chest. My, that's a fine show of muscle on them shoulders.'

Cribb stood up, nodding. 'Unusual development. Firm deltoids. A working-man's trade shows through his physique. Did you know that? Look at this now. A line like a tight-drawn cord between deltoids and biceps. Chances are that he's one of three – tanner, puddler or brickie.' He bent down again. 'Straight back, though. Puddling's not this one's trade. You recognize a puddler by the hump on his back, and that's muscle, not deformity. Newcastle's full of 'em.'

The old man professed interest in the anatomy lesson with a grunt. In fact, his stomach was beginning to lurch.

'Equal development of both arms cuts out smith's work or sawing,' continued Cribb. 'But when a man spends his day scraping hides or moving them around in the pits, he might grow like this. Could be a brickmaker, though. Let's look at the wrists. Moulding clay develops a brickie's forearm beautifully. Ah. Now this looks conclusive. Scars on the palms – probably from brick-edges, you see.' He turned the limb that he was examining, and whistled in surprise. 'Lord! Now this really is a symptom!'

Turning, he discovered his audience had abandoned him.

Edward Thackeray, Detective Constable, was not squeamish. He knew the London mortuaries as intimately as the pubs. If any reluctance was betrayed in his stride along Stamford Street towards Blackfriars mortuary on Tuesday it was not at the prospect of encountering the dead, but the quick, in the person of Sergeant Cribb. The order from the Yard to report to M Division headquarters had caught him unprepared the evening before. The news when he got there in the morning that he was to rendezvous with Cribb at Blackfriars confirmed his worst intimations. Barely eight months had elapsed since his transfer. Eight months of civilized service advising Hampstead stockbrokers how to secure their windows against burglars. The most taxing investigation of the period, an inquiry into an abducted heiress. Regular eight to six and no night duties. An inspector who was often out of the station for a week.

Now he was returning to Cribb. And a dismembered corpse in Blackfriars. Cribb, who ignored a man's age and susceptibility to irregular hours; who liked to account for every second of a constable's working day and then claim his sleeping-time as well.

Cribb had good points, of course. He might give you the treadmill treatment for days or weeks on end, but he let you know what part your work played in a case. If he was dour at times he also had spells – strange bouts of zest – when he glee-fully shared his pleasure at some small development. But at present it was not Cribb's better side that Thackeray was think-ing about.

He mounted the freshly scrubbed steps of the Hatfields work-house and passed through the building to the mortuary, a con-verted coach-house at the rear. His knock was answered by foot-steps inside and the sounds of an elaborate unlocking procedure. A mild-looking attendant – why one always expected something more sinister Thackeray was not sure – finally admitted the constable with a toss of the head. Sergeant Cribb was standing by his prize at a post-mortem table. From his expression he might have just gained a first at the local Flower Show.

'On time, Thackeray. Well done.'

'Morning, Sarge.'

'Good to have you with me again. There's a glum look about you, though. Depressing work in S Division, I suppose. Well that's over for a spell, I'm glad to tell you.'

The constable nodded philosophically, and Cribb continued his breezy small-talk. 'You've put on an inch or two about the waist, I see. Sure indication of reduced activity. Office work, eh?'

Typical of Cribb. Always ready with the personal slur.

'Not really, Sergeant. I've been busy enough with the work I've had. Old age, I suppose.' He studied Cribb's gaunt frame wishing he could honestly detect some flaw that was develop-ing, if it were only a receding hair-line or a stoop of the shoul-ders. The sergeant was in his forties and exasperatingly well-turned-out – neatly pressed suit, white wing collar, red spotted necktie. Cleanly trimmed Piccadilly Weepers, but no beard or moustache.

'The drape, if you please,' Cribb instructed the attendant,

and the body on the table was uncovered. 'What do you make of that, Thackeray?'

The constable moved to the table with interest, unaffected by the mutilation. Deep in concentration he spent three silent minutes over his examination.

'I would put death about four or five days ago, Sarge. Putrefaction ain't far advanced. He's obviously been hooked out of the river. Did Thames Division ask you to investigate?'

'Never mind that. What about the build?'

'Well, they're powerful arms and shoulders, all right. He's a labouring man, around forty years of age, I'd say. From the state of his palms he was probably a brickie.'

'Good. Injuries, apart from the obvious?'

'That was done with a cross-cut saw, I'm certain. But this bruising around the ribs is baffling, Sarge. And on the forearms. Must have been inflicted before death. I'd like to look at his back. Can we have him turned?' The attendant came forward. 'Thank you. Not much marking on this side. The grazing here looks as though it was done after death. Body likely struck something in the water.'

'What's your theory, then?' inquired Cribb.

Thackeray bent to the table again, and examined the right hand minutely, even sniffing at it for its secrets. He straightened, and shook his head.

'It makes no sense, Sarge.'

'What d'you mean?'

'These hands. Not the palms. The knuckle side. There's a pattern of old scars, and it ain't from brickmaking, I'm sure. No brickie's that careless with the backs of his hands. He's a well-built man, and his work's thickened his wrists, but that don't account for the size of his fist nor its coarseness. If it made any sense, Sarge, I'd say that hand's been pickled – soaked in vinegar, though you can't smell it any more. And scarred from knuckle-fighting.'

It was ridiculous, of course. Prize-fighting had been penalized out of existence twelve years before. But Cribb seemed satisfied with the diagnosis.

'Tidy thinking, Constable. Let's get outside, now. We'll walk back to the station.'

As they strolled, bowler-hatted, in the sunshine down Hatfields towards The Cut, Cribb talked with enthusiasm.

'He *must* be a pug. Everything's consistent. Body-bruising, scars, swollen hands. Even spike marks round the shins. And his trade. Brickmaking and scrapping have always gone together. Our man had a fight with the raw 'uns before he died, Thackeray. I'm sure of it.'

Thackeray was less convinced. 'It don't seem credible, Sarge. Prize-fighting's dead in England. The magistrates finished it in the sixties. Monstrous fines some of them promoters paid. When the railway excursions were banned that stopped it. They couldn't make it pay if no one went. It's all done with the gloves now. Endurance contests or Queensberry's rules.'

'Possibly it is, out Finchley way,' Cribb retorted, 'but you don't just stop a sport that's been established a century and a half. It's always been illegal under Common Law – Unlawful Assembly. But the fights went on, didn't they? Anyone that wanted could find out the venue – and get taken there in a special train.'

'I know that,' said Thackeray with a trace of petulance. 'And the magistrates would sometimes wait till a fight was over before they broke it up. I've stopped a few prize-fights myself in Essex when I was quite new to the Force. "The Blues!" they'd shout and before you got close the whole bloody scene would change in front of your eyes. All the paraphernalia – stakes, ropes, buckets, four-wheelers – just got moved a few fields away to another area, outside the authority of the local magistrates. Most fights came to a finish at some point even if they got interrupted. But I'm sure it don't go on now, Sergeant. *Bell's* hasn't reported a prize-fight for years, except in France or America, that is.'

'There's a rare amount going on that never reaches the Press,' commented Cribb. 'Prize-fighting might not offer the rewards it once did, when a promoter could wink at a magistrate, and

16

pugs like Sayers and Heenan and Mace were known to every cove that opened a newspaper. But there's still plenty who'll pay well to see a set-to with bare knuckles. Mittens haven't the same appeal.'

It occurred to Thackeray that his sergeant was displaying an unexpected working knowledge of pugilism. Almost, in fact, an affection for it. He decided not to comment.

'If our corpse does turn out to be a pug, Sarge, how do we find his identity? Who got him out of the river?'

'No help there. An old fishmonger. Showed me the body near Blackfriars Bridge. I questioned him, and believe he really did find it there.'

Thackeray accepted Cribb's judgement. Both knew that salvaging suicide victims from the Thames had become a minor industry. Once at safe anchorage a body could wait until a sufficiently generous reward was advertised by relatives. A patient professional would watch the papers day by day, and make his discovery only when the premium was right.

'How do we begin, then, Sergeant?'

Cribb was rarely at a loss. 'You begin at once, Constable. Take a walk across the Bridge to Fleet Street. See the boxing reporters. *Bell's* will be the first. Then the *Referee* and *The Sporting Life*. Extract anything you can about pugilism in London, on any scale at all. Make it quite plain you're not implicating them. That clear?'

'Yes, Sergeant.' Entirely clear. Cribb, as usual, keeping his subordinate occupied.

'And Thackeray.'

'Sergeant?'

'You might try the *Illustrated Sporting and Dramatic* office as well.'

For the second time in two days Cribb appeared that afternoon at Scotland Yard in the office of his Inspector. As initiator of this interview the sergeant was in buoyant mood. Jowett was plainly ill at ease. He had consented to seeing Cribb when an urgent appointment was requested. His subordinates rarely visited him voluntarily.

'Well, Sergeant. What's your business? Have you had second thoughts?'

Cribb enjoyed a moment's hesitation while the Inspector fumbled lighting his pipe.

'Not really, sir. It does relate to our conversation yesterday.'

'It does? You challenge my figures, perhaps?'

'Oh no,' Cribb reassured him. 'All quite accurate.'

'What is the problem, then?'

In the cab between Waterloo Road and Great Scotland Yard Cribb had rehearsed this conversation.

'No problem, sir. Merely seeking confirmation.'

'Are you, then? Confirmation of what?' The pipe was defying ignition.

'Something you told me yesterday. I want to put it into practical effect, sir.'

'Very good, Sergeant. I'm glad to hear that. But you need not refer everything to me, you know. My intention was to encourage initiative, not extinguish it.' Pleased at this pithy rejoinder, the Inspector relaxed a little, and propped the pipe on its stand in front of him. 'Since you're here, though, you may as well explain what is bothering you.'

'Bothering isn't quite the word, sir. You asked me to re-examine my methods of investigation.'

'Quite so. And you have?'

'In a manner of speaking, sir. Intuition, you said.'

'I most certainly did. And inspiration.'

'And flair, sir.'

'Good! And now you have a case, and you require guidance on the appropriate method of investigation.' Jowett intoned his words like a schoolmaster who has recognized a glimmer of intelligence in the class dunce.

'No, sir.'

The Inspector reached for his pipe.

'All I require from you, sir,' continued Cribb, 'is your agreement to a novel method of investigating a murder.'

'Novel ...? What exactly have you in mind, Sergeant?'

'I've reason for thinking a corpse found in my Division is that of a pugilist.'

'A boxer, you mean? That is the modern term, I believe.'

'No, sir. I mean a knuckle-fighter.'

Jowett frowned. 'But I don't understand you –'

'London Prize-Ring rules,' explained Cribb. 'No gloves. Supposed to have been stopped ten or more years ago. It goes on though. Not in my Division. Other parts of the city.'

'You're sure of this?'

'Can't ignore the evidence of a headless pug, sir. Clear signs of having scrapped in the last week or so. Without the mittens.' Cribb put his hands on the edge of the Inspector's desk and leaned forward confidentially. 'I'm taking this corpse very seriously, sir, very seriously indeed.'

'What do you mean?'

Cribb straightened and walked nonchalantly to the window. 'Passed an hour with the "Dead Persons Foul Play Suspected" lists this morning, sir. My dinner hour. Thought I'd remembered another headless one last January. I found it, and one more last year for the set, if you'll excuse a card-player's term. Each of 'em hooked out of the Thames, and both said to be very well-muscled. Could be pure chance, of course. Might be a pretty little pattern of murder among the fist-fighting mob, though.'

Jowett was shaking his head. 'I don't see how this can be true, Sergeant. Prize-fighting was carried on illegally a dozen years ago, as it had been for a century or more. But it was stopped by rigid enforcement, and has not been heard of since. It no longer commanded respect as a sport. You remember the ugly incidents, I expect. The fight between Sayers and that American –'

'Heenan, sir. The Benicia Boy.'

'Yes. It put pugilism in very bad odour. There was a damned regrettable episode at Fenchurch Street Station, too, when there was a brawl in the early hours of the morning.'

'The second Mace–King fight,' Cribb confirmed. 'End of 1862. The fault lay with the South Western Railway Company that

19

night. If they'd laid on sufficient trains in the first place the roughs would never have set about the ticket-holders.'

'I recall that it led to a good deal of criticism of the police,' said Jowett. 'Our point was, if I remember, that everyone present was engaged in an illegal activity so we bore no responsibility for those who were robbed and beaten, poor beggars.'

'That was it, sir. Even Jem Mace was struck. Bob Travers held the roughs off by using knuckle-dusters. Bill Richardson laid about them with the butt-end of a billiard cue.'

'You seem to have a vivid memory of the occasion, Sergeant.'

Cribb cleared his throat. 'Newspapers were full of it, sir.'

'Quite so. But really, Sergeant, I cannot say that I have heard much of prize-fighting since. A law was passed banning the special trains, I believe.'

'Regulations of Railways Act, 1868, sir,' barked Cribb. 'Section twenty-one. Imposed penalties of up to five hundred pounds.'

'Precisely.'

'Ah, but what goes on now doesn't involve trains. And it's all kept very close.'

'So you really think your corpse died in the prize-ring?'

'Can't say for certain, sir. He was a pug, though. And he had a fight shortly before death.'

'How do you know?'

'Pattern of bruising, sir. State of his knuckles.'

'Really? You seem to be quite an authority. Isn't yours a famous pugilistic name, now that I think of it?'

Cribb grinned tolerantly. 'Tom the Great? No connection, I'm sorry to admit. Ever seen his monument in Woolwich Old Church graveyard, sir? Sculptured from a twenty-ton block of Portland stone. You can see it from the Thames. Been some first-class men with the name of Cribb, sir, but only one has been commemorated on that scale.'

'Stop looking so damned wistful, Sergeant. Now, what's your business? I haven't time to discuss prize-fighting *or* your family.'

None the less his mood was more relaxed. If Jowett might be persuaded to concede anything, now was the moment.

Cribb spoke in earnest.

'I need to learn what's happening among the prize-fighting fraternity. I must get among them. Gain their confidence.'

'You need to be released from other duties for a time, you mean?'

'Certainly sir, but it's more than that. Fist-fighting's illegal. Always was. I may need to stand by while it goes on. Even appear to enjoy it.' As alarm coursed across the Inspector's face, Cribb added, 'French methods, you might say, sir.'

There was a significant pause.

'Can you really assure me that this is a necessary subterfuge, Sergeant?'

'Fundamental to my investigation, sir. Of course, if it's too unorthodox ...'

'Not at all –'

'Very good, sir. I presume, then, that Constable Thackeray can accompany me.'

Jowett blinked, scarcely aware that the decision was made. 'I – that is – yes.'

'Thank you, sir. We shan't actively encourage the pugs, I promise you.'

Jowett's jaw jolted. 'Indeed no! So far as this investigation is concerned, Sergeant, you must be meticulously cautious. Do nothing that smacks of conspiracy. That may be difficult in the circumstances, but you must abide by it. And I think it advisable, Sergeant, that you act without further reference to me in this case. You understand that if any of the divisional inspectors heard that one of my detectives had concealed information about illegal prize-fighting, for whatever reason, it might lead to a calamitous situation between this office and the Divisions.'

'Ruinous, sir,' agreed Cribb breezily.

Three minutes later he was striding in the sunshine along Whitehall. Jowett, alone at his desk, was obsessively drawing at his pipe.

Three

'It's been the same everywhere, Sarge. You mention fist-fighting, and they start. I've heard it all six times over this afternoon, from Gentleman Jackson to Jem Mace. Ropes and stakes, first bloods and knockdowns, fibbings and cross-buttocks until it fair turned my stomach. They all talk about the golden days with tears in their eyes until the ale runs out. But ask 'em where you might see a fist-fight nowadays and they look at you as if you was asking to meet Prince Albert, rest his soul.'

'You tried them all, then?'

'Except the *Referee* man. He was sacked six months ago because there wasn't enough scrapping of the gloved variety to keep him busy. They're all worried about their jobs, if you ask me.'

'Common complaint,' Cribb observed, thinking of Scotland Yard. 'Did you ask what happened to the promoters and backers? They can't all have vanished.'

'Seems they turned to other sports, Sarge. The turf, or pedestrianism. There ain't the money in glove-fighting.'

They paced the Victoria Embankment, watching the river traffic. It was too warm to be indoors. Thackeray needed air, anyway, after his spell on duty in the bars of Fleet Street. Ahead of them two small boys chased metal hoops. The glittering Thames seemed totally innocent of anything so unpoetic as a headless corpse.

'Jago,' said Cribb.

'What's that, Sarge?'

'Henry Jago. He's the young cove to see. Should have thought of it before.'

'Another newspaperman?' inquired Thackeray.

'Someone much more useful. A constable. Young fellow attached to the Yard. Come on, Thackeray. If we're in luck he may be off duty.'

Cribb set off at a brisk pace towards Northumberland Avenue. Thackeray, reacting less quickly, followed a few paces behind and toppled a straying hoop in his efforts to close with the sergeant.

'Fungus face!' bawled the owner.

At Palace Place, Great Scotland Yard, Cribb marched up to the building known in the Department as 'single men's quarters'. P.C. Jago had a room on the second floor, and they noisily mounted an uncarpeted staircase.

'This Jago,' queried Thackeray, rather short of breath.

'Yes?'

'Has he made a study of prize-fighting?'

'Better than that,' said Cribb. 'He's a first-class boxer.'

They stood by a door on the second-floor landing. It was dark indoors after the July sunshine. Thackeray peered closely at a small white rectangle mounted in brass on the door.

'Blimey, Sarge. A visiting card! "Henry Jago. Constable, Metropolitan Police." Can you credit that? First time I've seen such a thing in nearly thirty years in the Force! Why, I don't suppose even Inspector Jowett's got one. "Constable, Metropolitan Police"!'

Cribb sniffed. 'Keep your voice down. Don't want to give him offence. Jago's from a high-class family. Private tutor and public school. Should have gone to University. Certainly had the money for it. There was some sort of family quarrel, though. Young Jago walked out in protest and joined the Force.'

'Good Lord!' exclaimed Thackeray, who had never encountered such a well-connected constable.

'Hope he's in.' Cribb knocked.

Nothing.

A second knock.

Sounds from inside.

A pause.

The door opened a few inches and Constable Jago's eyes appeared through the gap.

'What the – Sergeant Cribb! Come in, gentlemen.'

The door swung inwards and revealed a figure in a striped cotton nightshirt.

'You must excuse me. Working at nights, you understand. Do

find yourselves a chair. You'll think me most uncivil, but I cannot offer you a drink. I try to avoid all intoxicants, and I can't endure the torment of keeping them for guests. Perhaps an orange?'

The visitors declined, and waited while Jago drew back the curtains and straightened the bed he had just left. Sturdily built and in his early twenties, he moved about with remarkable agility for one who had been slumbering two minutes before.

He left the room to wash. Thackeray got up to examine the mantelshelf. 'Blondin poised on his wire above Niagara', a well-thumbed postcard in a picture-frame, held the position of honour between two pewter boxing trophies. An antique chiming clock had been moved aside, and crowned with soiled collars.

Thackeray crossed the room to a book-case stacked with piles of sporting newspapers weighted down by odd dumb-bells and the two standard volumes on criminal law. What caught his eye, resting on top, was a half-filled decanter.

'I thought he said he didn't keep liquor.'

'What is it?' asked Cribb.

Thackeray removed the glass stopper and took a deep, speculative sniff. He instantly regretted doing so.

'Elliman's,' announced Cribb. 'Can smell it from here. Embrocation. Splendid for toning the muscles. Not recommended by the glass.'

Thackeray produced a large handkerchief and cleared his nostrils. He joined Cribb on the sofa just as Jago re-entered, now presentable in shirt and regulation trousers.

'We haven't cut into your sleep too much, I hope?' inquired Cribb, in a whim of compassion.

'Not at all, Sergeant. I'm due to report at five.'

'Good. You keep up the sporting interest, I see.'

'Yes, in my spells off duty.' Jago's accent was impeccable.

'Handsome portrait, that.' Cribb was looking at a large framed engraving of Captain Matthew Webb that hung above the bed.

'A great man, Sergeant.'

'Yes, indeed. Headed in the right direction, too.'

Both constables were baffled by Cribb's remark.

'Dover to Calais. France, you see. The modern man goes to France for fresh ideas, or so I'm told. Remember that when you next meet Inspector Jowett. How's the boxing, Jago?'

'Oh, I try to keep up with it, Sergeant, but they keep me busy here.'

'Let's see. You won a medal at the Police Tournament last winter, and damned near collected a Queensberry Cup as well, didn't you?'

'Some did say I was unlucky to lose the middleweight title, Sergeant.'

'So I heard. Where d'you train?'

A look of concern came into Jago's eyes.

'Here mostly, Sergeant. I've got the dumb-bells, you see, and a chest-expander –'

'Sparring they call it, don't they?' broke in Cribb. 'Practising with other boxers. Where d'you do it?'

'I . . .' He clenched his hands in front of him and regarded them uneasily. Police Regulation 3 seemed written across them. *Members of the Force are ordered at all times to lead an orderly private life and keep respectable company.*

'This isn't trouble,' Cribb reassured him. 'I need your help. If you know any of the fist-fighting fraternity you may help me find a killer. Where do you go to train?'

Jago replaced his hands in his pockets.

'There's a public house near Covent Garden, Sergeant. The Anchor. It has a large room attached to it. The landlord had it fitted out as a gym. Most of the boxing men in London know it.'

'Fist-fighters?'

Jago gulped. 'Good heavens, no! It's strictly a glove-fighting establishment – not exactly the Athenaeum, you understand, but there are certain limitations on the membership. Some of the attendants may be ex-pugilists, from what I've heard, but I don't actually associate with them.'

'Really?' Breeding will out, thought Cribb wryly. 'Ever heard talk of prize-fighting going on these days?'

'Yes. There are those who hint at it. A whisper goes round that there's sport to be had in some quiet corner of Kent or Essex, and a party's got up to make an excursion. It's not partridge or pheasant those characters go to find, Sergeant. But I think it prudent to close my ears to such talk.'

'You've heard nothing of the fights themselves. No names?'

'No, but if I showed interest –'

'Do they know you're in the Force?'

Jago gave thought to the question. His thinking processes were markedly less agile than Cribb's.

'I don't arrive in my uniform, and I most certainly avoid conversation about my duties. It's possible that someone has heard of my matches in the Police Tournament, but I rather doubt that. They don't treat me with the suspicion that one customarily encounters.'

'Good. When are you next going to the Anchor?'

'Tomorrow at lunch-time was the next training session I planned. There are usually several sparring partners available around noon. I limber for thirty minutes or so, and then have half a dozen rounds with whoever is there. A most interesting assortment of men find their way there. Military officers, undergraduates, members of the Stock Exchange –'

'You know their professions,' Cribb rapped out. 'What's to prevent them from knowing yours?'

'I keep it to myself, Sergeant. If they ask, I say I'm engaged in clerical work at Whitehall. Which I am, more's the pity.'

Cribb was satisfied. He had harboured reservations about Jago's ability to carry out detective work.

'Very well. If you want action I can arrange it. From tomorrow onwards you'll be working for me, and your duties will start at the Anchor. I need information about prize-fighting and you're the man to seek it out – names, places, times. Handle this carefully. Listen, rather than interrogate, but don't be reluctant to show interest. Are you game?'

Henry Jago was game, and Sergeant Cribb left at once to arrange his transfer to M Division.

To a field on the Moat Farm, a mile north of Rainham on the Southend Road, came three strangers. They carried a length of rope looped around the shoulders of the tallest, a bundle of stakes and a mallet. After agitated discussion and pointing of hands they approached a patch of ground more even than the rest. Watched by a trio of interested sheep, they paced the shape of a square in earnest concentration. Four of the stakes were distributed at the corners and one was driven securely into the earth. The rope was attached to it, and played out to a length of about eight yards, previously marked on the rope with white paint. The position for the second stake was measured and marked, but it was not fixed in the ground. Nor were the other two, although their points were used to make shallow holes in the turf. When this surveying exercise was complete the men carried stakes, ropes and mallet to the hedge bordering the field and secreted them in the longer grass there. Their business completed, they returned towards Rainham.

Two full days passed. Thackeray was sent to ask questions of the clientele in a list of public houses famous for their boxing promotions, from the Swan at Upper Clapton to the Marquis of Granby at Lambeth. All he learned was the Queensberry Rules and the potency of wines in wood. Jago sparred at the Anchor gymnasium until his ribs ached, and talked into the small hours with the trainers there. He learned the roll of champions from Figg to Mace. Sergeant Cribb attended an inquest on the headless pugilist and learned that he died from causes unknown. 'The medical witnesses have not established indisputably that this unfortunate man died as the result of his beheading,' the coroner had said. 'True, the post-mortem revealed no other cause of death, but until and unless the head of this corpse can be located, the post-mortem is not conclusive.'

The news of a prize-fight arranged for Friday evening at a venue in Essex finally came not from one of Jago's trainers, but from the stationmaster at Fenchurch Street.

'He frequents the gym at lunch-times to practise lifting weights,' Jago explained to Cribb. 'I believe he's endeavouring to reduce his waistline. I scarcely know the fellow, but he overheard me asking somebody whether pugilism could ever be revived – an indirect method of inquiry, you see, Sergeant – and he quite openly told me that he knew of a fight this coming Friday night. He says that he can tell by the advance purchase of railway tickets. I inquired how he knew that it was not a gloved contest and he told me that the day one of the Fancy endures a train journey to, pardon the expression, see a bloody waltz with muffs on hasn't come yet, and in his opinion never would.'

So Cribb and his two assistants waited stolidly in rich Essex mud surrounding the freshly erected ring at the Moat Farm. The conditions were not ideal for outdoor sport. Rain had spotted the windows when the train reached Barking. At Rainham when they disembarked there was a deluge. It lessened in intensity as the three hundred pilgrims paddled along a lane running with water. Twenty minutes later when they reached the ring there was a soft but insistent drizzle.

'Regulation boots! They let the water in like ruddy sluicegates,' Thackeray complained to Jago.

'Should have come prepared, like me,' Cribb intervened. 'Never visit the country without galoshes and a waterproof. Antipluvium, this one. Excellent value. Hello! There's action at last.'

Thackeray was distracted from his sodden feet by a commotion at one of the corners. A cap was tossed into the ring. A large figure ducked between the ropes. A hulk, far larger than Cribb's headless corpse, retrieved the cap. Cheers from a few supporters. The response: a generous deposit of spittle where the cap had lain.

'Meanix!' announced several who knew. 'The Stepney Ox!'

To murmurs of awe Mr Meanix toured the ring, scowling at the patrons, and finally returned to his corner and produced a scarlet square of silk from his pocket. This he looped around one of the stakes. A supporter wrapped an overcoat around his shoulders. He shrugged it off and it dropped to the mud at his feet. It was humbly retrieved from under the lower rope. Meanix waited, statuesque, skin gleaming with moisture, trying to seem oblivious to the din around him.

'Ever seen him at the Anchor?' Cribb asked Jago.

28

'Good gracious, no, Sergeant. He's not the class of man we encourage.'

There was no indication anywhere of an opponent for the Ox. Bookies snaking among the crowd were already taking bets freely, regardless that no one seemed sure who would be the second pugilist. There were copious suggestions, ranging from names well known in the amateur ring to former champions whose age would give them scant chance against Meanix.

'How does a man like that keep in trim?' Thackeray inquired. 'If the Anchor wouldn't admit him, where could he take his breathings?'

'There's places that would,' said Cribb. 'Lambeth School of Arms is one. Filthy, evil-smelling hole. I was there last Wednesday. Great barn of a place with a ring set up inside. Crowds packed in like herrings. And smelling like 'em. Every inch of room taken. Even up in the rafters I could see young street-arabs. Must have got in through the roof somehow. That's Meanix's setting.'

'What was the fighting like?'

'Barely within the law. Gloves plainly had the horsehair taken out. Time-keeping was variable according to the state of the fighting. Queensberry's Rules, they announced at the outset, and then had a four-minute round followed by two under two minutes when there were knockdowns.'

'Couldn't that kind of place be where our man was beaten to death?'

'Unlikely,' said Cribb. 'State of his hands wasn't consistent with glove-fighting of any sort. Besides, the fighters there have too strong a following. Regular clientele. You couldn't drop one of them off Waterloo Bridge without someone raising a barney. Now this little set-to here is a far likelier invitation to violence. Crowd out from London, more set on placing a pretty bet than following a pug's fortunes. Meanix may be known to a few, but who'd miss him if he dropped dead here in front of us? None of this mob is going to report the fact. You don't risk prosecution to report the passing of a knuckle fighter who means no more to you than a guinea at five to one.'

The pleasure of anticipation was perceptibly waning among the spectators. With the initial stakes placed, the betting could not hold much interest until Meanix's opponent appeared. They took to looking about them, examining their neighbours, half expecting anyone of better-than-average build to disrobe and duck under the ropes. Cribb nudged young Jago, winked and tilted his head fractionally towards the vacant corner. Thackeray noticed this, and saw the flash of momentary uncertainty in the constable's eyes. The sergeant had found a new subject for his dubious wit.

In the ring even Meanix was betraying unease. He crossed his arms to massage his biceps, searching the faces of the crowd who stood near.

'Here they come!' The general mutterings stopped. Three riders approached at a canter across the field, raising a small mist of water-vapour from the saturated turf. The interest shifted from Meanix to the newcomers. Volunteers ran forward to hold the horses as they were reined, steaming, some distance from the ring. The riders dismounted, a dandified figure in ulster, black boots and top hat, and two younger men, massively built, one a Negro. He began to strip.

'Seven to four against the Ebony!' shouted a bookie, and the betting resumed in earnest.

'He'll be the local champion,' Cribb explained. 'The challenger is Meanix. He had to toss his cap into the ring first.'

'The betting goes with Meanix, even so,' remarked Thackeray. 'He carries too much top hamper for the Ebony to fell him.'

'We'll see.'

A minute or so later the Ebony joined the Ox in the ring, bare-chested, and in striking white boxing-drawers fastened at mid-calf level. His swarthy muscularity drew whistles of genuine admiration from the ringside. If Meanix was an ox here was a panther.

Now to a riot of abuse and booing, Meanix's two attendants ducked under the rope and reported to the referee, a pale man in muffler and cap who had appeared from nowhere. He seemed well enough known, and proved to be a Rainham innkeeper. The weighings, he announced, to those who could hear, had shown a stone and a quarter in favour of Meanix at fourteen stone seven. Were the colours in position?

The larger of the Ebony's attendants hustled forward with a square of black silk, which he tied above Meanix's scarlet kerchief on one of the centre stakes. A toss was made for corners. Meanix selected the one his attendants had already claimed.

'Will seconds and bottle-holders now withdraw?'

Even the referee left the ring.

'Time.'

They walked to the centre and crossed hands, glowering menace at each other.

'Go to it, Ox,' bawled a bystander.

The fight began.

The shifting mass of umbrellas and hats surrounding the small square of green jerked to stillness. It crystallized into hundreds of faces, regularly spaced, each distinct in character. Every moustache, beard, cigar came into focus. Every eye was fastened on the pugilists. They, firm in the classical stance, faced each other, probing the space between them with hard-clenched fists. For a time the impact of rain on umbrella-silk was almost the only sound. Then, with the preliminary measuring up complete, the patrons began to demand action.

Meanix ventured a left arm, the Ebony swayed out of range, and shouts of encouragement descended on them from all sides. Two or three flicking movements from Meanix's leading arm failed to connect with the bobbing Negro, who showed no aggression. Responding to the impatient cries of his following, Meanix advanced several inches with a simultaneous heel-toe movement of both feet, rather as a fencer progresses. Then he brought his right fist above his shoulder and swung it violently towards his opponent's face. It was an obvious punch, and easily parried, but he followed it with a stabbing left thrust that found its mark on the Ebony's belly. Then Meanix closed, butting his head hard into his man's chest and wrapping his arms around the torso. With a swift lunge forward of his right leg and a simultaneous jerk he swung the Negro against the bridge made by his thigh and toppled him. To a warm ovation the first round was over.

'First knockdown to the Ox,' said Thackeray with significance. The fight would not last long in his opinion.

'He's a redoubtable fellow,' agreed Jago.

Cribb was watching the Ebony, who stood in his corner while his attendant wiped mud from his arms.

Half a minute was allowed between rounds. At a signal from the referee the pair squared up again, and soon began to exchange strenuous punches, the Negro giving as good as he received. Red patches began to colour Meanix's chest, where it had received the Ebony's attention. A sudden crash of heads jolted both men and for a few seconds, as if by mutual consent, they wrestled against the ropes and then crashed together to the grass.

The following two rounds were brief and uneventful, both ending with Meanix back-heeling his rival. The bookies in the crowd tried to revive interest in the odds at each break between rounds, but they were doing poor business.

'Everyone waits for first blood,' Cribb explained. 'Watch the rush to bet when the claret flows.'

It happened in the fifth round. Meanix caught the Ebony squarely on the nose.

'Scarlet as a geranium. What d'you think of that?' declared one of their neighbours. 'As sweet a punch as I've seen! Plant one on 'is peepers, Meanix.'

Without quite managing that, the Ox succeeded in felling his wounded rival with a swinging blow to the ear. The Ebony's seconds hauled him to the corner. There he sat on one attendant's arched thigh, while the other staunched the flow from his nose.

'That's the kind of blow that tells,' said Cribb. 'A good fist-fighter will touch up the listeners as often as he's able. It's an art that died when glove-fighting came in. If you've ever felt a man's raw 'uns about your ears you'll know what I mean.'

For the next six rounds the Ox repeatedly battered his rival to his knees, several times falling heavily across him to add to the effect. The betting, which had never favoured the Ebony, was now heavily against him. Meanix had not once resorted to his second's knee between rounds.

'No sort of mill at all, this,' declared Thackeray with a superior air. 'They shouldn't have brought a novice out to face the Londoner. He hasn't fairly grassed Meanix once.'

'There's time enough,' Cribb pointed out. 'The black's scarce marked as yet. Meanix has the edge on the pulley-hawley work, but it won't count for much in a fight to the finish. There's steam in the Ebony.'

Almost as if in response to this tribute the Negro rose to the referee's next call and began to counter-assault, plainly surprising Meanix. A well-directed left caught the Ox in the throat as he lumbered forward incautiously. A second jab with the same fist split his lip.

'On the ivories!' shouted one of the crowd.

Meanix put the back of his right hand to the bleeding mouth. It was an instinctive movement, to check for blood. Unfortunately for him it left his body unguarded. A lightning blow caught him in the stomach, and he dropped like a stone.

'Beautiful! On the mark!' called the admirer. Now it was the turn of Meanix's seconds to drag him clear and revive him with sal volatile.

'The mark?' queried Thackeray.

'Point of the stomach. Known as Broughton's mark,' Cribb explained. 'One of the classic punches.'

Meanix had scarcely recovered when the end of the thirty seconds was called. The seconds heaved him upright and pushed him heftily towards his punisher.

'Now we'll see if there's any science to the Ebony,' Cribb said, in some excitement. 'Any hawbuck fighter can fell a man. It takes class to keep him upright while you dose him.'

Class it was that the Ebony displayed, for the round lasted six minutes, and Meanix was hit with every variety of punch. Some in the crowd delightedly classified each blow in the *patois* of pugilism: 'On the ivories!' 'Whisker!' 'Liver hit!' 'On the mark!' 'Peepers!' Others, more materialistic, sought out the bookmakers to cover their losses. The Ebony continued efficiently with his work, concentrating punches on the swollen areas of flesh around Meanix's eyes and mouth. There was no need now for crude hammer-blows; he hit with the cutting edge of the fist, the sharply angled central joints of the clenched fingers, lancing the swellings with a surgeon's precision, in short, swift stabs. When specks of blood showed at five or six points he stood back to survey the work. Then, as Meanix blundered against the ropes, the Ebony attacked again with harder blows, broadening the incisions to free-flowing gashes, until lines of crimson patterned Meanix's face and chest. Once Meanix threatened to overbalance, and the Negro hugged him maternally until he was sufficiently stable to take the next volley of blows. They were aimed at the mouth and jowls, which must have been particularly sore, for Meanix actually made a pathetic parrying movement before backing to the nearest corner. There he waited, leaning hard on the corner-stake, his open hands raised to protect the wounds on his face. Instead the attack came in a series of cruel blows to the ribs. He bowed in agony, quite open now to an upper-cut that would have settled the match. But the Ebony had other plans. He gripped his opponent under the chin and led him like the ox he was claimed to resemble to the centre of the ring. Then with astonishing agility he turned his back on Meanix and upended him over his thigh in a perfect cross-buttock.

Meanix lasted one round more. His attendants miraculously got him to the vertical position in the half-minute, but he was semi-conscious when he lurched out. One eye was closed and the other half blinded with mud and gore. His bloated lips slobbered blood and saliva. In the corner he had spat out two teeth into the slop-bucket. One blow finished the fight. A long, low jab in the diaphragm. He doubled forward and plummeted to the mud.

The sponge was tossed in beside him.

Four

The four-square semblance of order ended. One side-stake leaned inwards under pressure and a corner-post collapsed simultaneously. The ropes slackened and fell and the ring was a thoroughfare. In seconds the only indication of a fight being staged there was the glistening head and shoulders of the Ebony, clear among the umbrellas surrounding him. Altogether larger groups converged on the bookies. Many customers, it seemed, had succeeded in hedging their bets before the result was completely obvious. Professional gamblers, they needed to be as sensitive to the state of a fight as a broker to the stock market.

'Short fight,' commented Cribb, 'and small entertainment to it.'

'Fourteen rounds. Fifty-three minutes by my half-hunter,' said Thackeray in confirmation. 'Have you ever boxed that long, Henry?'

Jago had not. The brutality of what they had seen appeared to have affected him, for he was deathly pale. 'That wasn't boxing. That wasn't sport at all.'

'You mean that there's more footwork in glove-fighting?' suggested Thackeray. 'I suppose if they put spiked shoes on you and stood you ankle-deep in mud you might go as sluggishly as those two did in the early rounds. You could last an hour of that, couldn't you?'

Jago shuddered. It could have been from the cool of the evening.

Cribb pulled the collar of the waterproof against his side-whiskers and did not even look at Jago. 'Three hours,' he said, tersely.

'Three hours, Sergeant?' asked Jago.

'The time you should allow for a fist-fight, lad. Plenty go to two hours and some have gone to four.'

Jago did not pretend to be an expert on pugilism. He left that to Cribb. No right-minded bobby questioned his sergeant's authority on any subject.

'What happened to the beaten man?' asked Thackeray. He had been engrossed in pressing rainwater from his beard on to a large linen handkerchief.

'A sharp-eyed detective would have seen,' replied Cribb, equally uncomfortable in the conditions. 'If you can manage to bend your waist a fraction you'll see him lying where the other man put him.'

'Still there? What's happened to his attendants?'

'Looking for browns. Some were tossed in after he went down. It's the only purse Meanix gets tonight. The crowd's thinning now. Let's go closer.'

They moved through churned mud where the ringsiders had been and across the fallen ropes to the protected greener square. Only the centre patch was black and glutinous. On it lay the Stepney Ox, oblivious to the legs stepping across him. There too was one of his seconds, crouching, not to raise him, but to salvage a halfpenny from under his forearm.

'He's breathing,' observed Jago, with some relief.

'One less for Waterloo Bridge, then,' murmured Thackeray.

Cribb addressed the scavenging second. 'When are you returning to London?'

The face turned. It was scarred by years of fist-fighting. One eye was sightless, stilled, perhaps, by an opponent's thumb.

'What's it to you?'

Cribb produced a coin and held it between finger and thumb above the expanse of Meanix's back. It was a satisfactory answer.

'Last train. We'll bring 'im round at the Fox in Rainham. Time enough to spend what we've picked up 'ere. Too bloody tight-fisted, this lot are. Don't give credit for a rousing scrap. Ah! I'm obliged to you, guv.'

The spectators were by now steadily dispersing. Most headed in the direction of Rainham, and the railway station. The referee, clearly determined for his own reasons to be first away, was already visible above a distant hedgerow, pedalling his fifty-inch Coventry Perfection dextrously through the rutted lanes towards the Fox and Grapes.

'We'll go the same way,' Cribb announced. 'I'm ready for refreshment.'

They joined the general trek, leaving Meanix and a small entourage. The beaten pugilist had managed to struggle to his feet, and was now wrapped in a horse-blanket. The victor and his companion were evidently not joining the group at Rainham. They had already left, walking their horses slowly in the direction from which they had come.

The Fox (no one found it necessary to mention the Grapes as well) was a small inn, conveniently close to Rainham station. Well before the detectives reached there, the influx from London had arrived and begun the process of obliterating their memory of the fight. Cribb edged a passage to the counter with difficulty and ordered three glasses of porter. Thackeray had found a single seat under a window, towards which Cribb moved with the tankards, ducking to avoid an oil-lamp slung from a beam.

'Doesn't look as strong as it might,' he said, accepting the chair, 'but anything's welcome when you've got a thirst.'

'Been to th' fight, 'ave you?'

The speaker was one of a group of eight firmly established around the three sides of the window-seat. From the style and dry state of their dress they were the local clientele, alone among those present in not having been at Moat Farm.

Cribb nodded. 'You didn't go, then?'

There were superior smiles all round.

'Standin' in 'Arrison's field for an hour or more, watchin' the Ebony alter a London bruiser's profile? We got better ways o' passin' time, friend.'

'You're not betting men, then?' inquired Thackeray, to encourage the conversation.

'Bettin'?' The speaker, shrewd behind his grey whiskers, with squirrel-sharp eyes that darted meaningfully around the table before each remark, added, 'Bettin' ain't part o' God's law. And God in 'Is mercy preserves us from temptation by keepin' down our wages to what we can spend in 'ere. 'Ow long did y' London man last, then?'

'Fourteen rounds.'

'Hm. Fair showing.' The nodding of heads around the table showed a striking consensus of agreement. 'What was the odds before they started?'

'Strongly favouring Meanix,' said Cribb. 'If we'd known the black was so handy with his dukes, we'd have made a few pounds tonight.'

'Ebony's form ain't broadly known,' agreed the spokesman. 'We know 'im round these parts, o' course. I'm told that if fist-fights was still written up in th' papers you London folk would've 'eard of 'im afore now. Don't really trouble us, as only Ben there can read, and 'e prefers 'is prayer-book to sportin' news, don't you, mate?'

Smiles were liberally exchanged.

'Has the Ebony fought many in Rainham, then?' Cribb inquired.

'Only two that I know of. Both was said to 'ave their record in *Fistiana* – though we wouldn't know that, would we, mates, bein' illiterate men? Ebony sledge-'ammered 'em both.'

'When was this?'

'Lor', now you've asked me somethin'. The memory ain't tickin' over so well. Strikes me it needs a spot o' lubrication. What d'you say, mates?'

They said nothing, but drained their glasses simultaneously.

Cribb saw what had to be done. Jago and Thackeray followed him to the bar with handfuls of empty glasses. There Thackeray felt it his duty to caution the sergeant.

'They're not truthful men, Sarge. It's not worth standing them drinks when their word ain't reliable.'

'I'll judge that,' said Cribb. 'Let 'em have their sport with us. I can pick wheat from chaff.'

When the first sips had been taken, Cribb again put his question about the Ebony's previous fights.

'I'll give it some thought, mate. Last November, I reckon, was when 'e fought that Bermondsey boy.'

There was general concurrence.

'And the Webster fight was two months back, easy. Around Easter, that was.'

If this could be believed, Thackeray inwardly noted, the headless corpse could not be Mr Webster's.

'This Ebony,' Cribb persisted, 'seems a stout fighter. Who trains him?'

The spokesman shook his head.

'Can't say we know much about 'im, mate, save that 'e's a capital bruiser.'

'Where does he live, then? I'd like to meet the fellow.'

This was hilariously received. The spokesman explained why.

'Ebony comes from Vibart's place, Radstock 'All, a mile or more north of the village. And they don't much like strangers up there, 'cept the ones they invite.'

'You mean that they don't enter into village life?'

'In a manner of speaking. We see 'em once in a while. The Ebony, just as you saw 'im today. Sometimes Mrs Vibart in 'er four-wheeler, or the menfolk 'eadin' for London, or comin' back. But they're none of 'em conversationalists, if you follow me.'

'This Vibart,' said Cribb. 'What does he do?'

'Do?'

'What's his work?'

There was more amusement at this.

'Mr Vibart ain't really fit for work any more, mate. You see, 'e's been dead this twelvemonth.'

'Really? Was he old, then?'

'Far from it. I could give 'im twenty year, and I'm still capable in all particulars. Jacob there could give 'im fifty, and all 'e's lost is a few ivories, ain't it, Jacob?'

Jacob revealed a pink mouth in confirmation.

'You mentioned menfolk at the Hall,' persisted Cribb. 'Are they servants?'

'Training-folk. They're none of 'em local men, I can tell you. Oh, and there's Vibart's brother, Edmund. We see Edmund at least once a week bein' devout men, don't we, Ben?'

Ben swore passionately and everyone chuckled.

'Edmund Vibart's our church organist, you see. And a very

fine lead 'e gives to our singin' of the psalms. Yes, a rare musician is Mr Vibart, a very upright member of the church.'

'Really? But you said they didn't enter into village life.'

'Ah, did I now? Well, I wouldn't really call Edmund a village man, you know. As I say, we see 'im in church on Sundays, those of us that go to Sung Eucharist and Matins, but you ain't liable to see 'im any other time, unless it's passin' in a carriage. 'E don't call on us for a yarn and a smoke any more than we'd look 'im up at Radstock 'All.'

'You've never been inside, then?'

'Not since the Vibarts moved in. None of us go up there now. Mrs Vibart wanted maids, but she couldn't get no Rainham wenches to stop there.'

'Why should that be?'

'Oh, no good reason you could name. Wenches' talk, mostly. Strange things 'appenin' there, that grow in the tellin', no doubt. Though there ain't much you could tell some of our lasses, eh, mates?'

Even Thackeray and Jago were now attuned to the ponderous local wit, and joined in the broad winks.

There was one more question Cribb wanted to put.

'Is the Ebony the only fist-fighter at Radstock Hall?'

It seemed to unsettle the spokesman. His companions, too, stopped smiling.

'We've talked enough about Rainham folk,' he said, after a pause. 'Now you can tell us about London. 'Ave you seen the Crystal Palace?'

The mood relaxed, and Radstock Hall was dropped from the conversation. It was not mentioned again in the Fox that night. And after the marvels of the Crystal Palace were summed up in three short sentences by Cribb, he offered a more familiar glimpse of London life. With artistry nurtured in M Division smoking concerts, he impersonated a street tragedian in the Strand contesting his pitch with a German band. Thackeray then took the stage with a hilarious impression of Irving having an off-night in *The Bells*. Jago's contribution began with a colourful account of street entertainers, from performing dogs to fire-eating Indians. From there it was an easy progression to rope-tricks, and so to his favourite topic, 'the Automaton of the Age, Blondin'. At this point he placed his glass on the table and rose to demonstrate. A line between the floorboards became the tightwire suspended above the stage of the Royal Polytechnic. Pago edged agonizingly across, seesawing his outstretched arms in a beautifully convincing performance.

A sudden shout from the end of the room of 'Blimey, the train!' returned everyone to reality except Jago. Totally absorbed in his balancing, he heard the shout, swayed alarmingly, flailed the air with his arms and crashed to the floor. This in no way interrupted the general scramble for the door. The London train was due, and nobody wanted to spend the night in Rainham. The more sober stepped over the fallen artiste. Others were less fastidious.

'They're right,' Thackeray confirmed. 'Ten-fifty. We must get to the station.'

Cribb had been silent for some time; not from rapture at Jago's performance.

'Not us,' he muttered tersely. 'Jago goes. We stay.'

Constable Jago, now sheepishly brushing mud from his Norfolk, looked up in surprise.

'We'll see you out, lad,' Cribb continued; and then, for the benefit of the others, 'Do excuse us, gentlemen. Must get our young friend on to the train.'

He pushed the puzzled constable ahead of him to the door. Outside they could talk more freely.

'You must travel with Meanix and the London mob. Get close enough to listen to 'em. I've got business here with Thackeray. We'll take the first train back in the morning. Report to the station at nine tomorrow. I expect to be there. If I'm not, tell the Inspector everything that happened. And ask him, at my request, to get a squad of picked men out to Radstock Hall.'

A minute later, still in some bewilderment, Jago was seated in the same carriage as the now-intoxicated Stepney Ox, bound for London.

*

Perhaps it appealed to Cribb's sense of humour, forcing a man in his fifties across drenched fields in Essex, half an hour before midnight. It was possible, Thackeray speculated, that if *he* had gallivanted about the bar of the Fox like a penguin attempting flight Cribb might have sent *him* back to a warm bed in London. He suffered because he was utterly dependable.

As though he read the constable's thoughts, Cribb explained, 'Far better for young Jago to keep a watch on Meanix and his friends. He's more the Corinthian than you or I. Should be up to bandying talk of milling with that contingent, and might hear a useful word or two besides. You don't mind a spot of night duty?'

'No, Sarge,' lied Thackeray. He felt his left boot sink into a hollow. Water seeped through his sock. 'But I begin to wonder whether we're still on course. We haven't passed so much as a shack this last half-hour, and there's no sign of buildings ahead. I can't say that I trusted that group in the pub. To be frank, Sarge, I can picture them back there somewhere laughing over our short cut.'

'That may be so,' conceded Cribb. 'But our direction isn't far wrong, even if the going ain't exactly Pall Mall. We're following the same course the Ebony and his friend took. I don't take the word of a bunch of swivel-eyed rustics without checking for myself.'

One consolation was that the rain-clouds were fast dispersing, and there were frequent short periods of moonlight. Between them huge shadows traversed the fields like black tides. The landscape was depressingly flat, relieved only by a few small silhouetted copses. Thackeray tried to put the grinning rustics out of his mind. He concentrated on planting each step on the most solid ground available.

'There's a chimney!' announced Cribb in some triumph fifteen minutes later. 'Above the cedars there. Unmistakable.'

They cut across a turnip crop, quickening their pace. As they approached the group of trees that increasingly dominated the landscape a lane was revealed, snaking in from the right.

'There's the approach road,' Cribb announced. 'Look where it comes from. Would have added miles to our walk.'

Thackeray never openly questioned his sergeant's infallibility. But he noted with satisfaction that Cribb's right galosh was missing, claimed by some quagmire they had passed through.

The estate of Radstock Hall was enclosed by a six-foot wall. This the detectives surmounted with the help of an overhanging branch. Their progress was deliberate and by no means stealthy. Instinctively they felt secure from guards, dogs or other hazards the grounds might contain. The trees and scrub were dense enough, anyway, to give them cover if necessary. The house was moonlit when they reached it. An elegant Elizabethan country house in glimmering red-brick. The roof, still damp from the earlier downpour, gleamed theatrically. Gaunt, well-weathered chimneys jutted against the restless sky.

They skirted the building, moving with more caution now, and keeping in the shadow of the foliage, although no lights were burning at the front. As they rounded the side of the house Cribb stopped abruptly and said, almost aloud, 'God Almighty!'

Thackeray froze. His sergeant was not given to casual blasphemy. Around the corner was something exceedingly unpleasant. A procession of headless corpses would not have provoked a more extreme outburst. But the horror confronting Thackeray when he looked was altogether different. Not a physical violation at all, but an aesthetic one. With blatant disregard to the style of the house a squat, grey, modern wing had been added to the back, as vulgar as a blow-fly on a rose. What sort of people were these?

'Take it slow now,' cautioned Cribb. 'We'll get a closer look if we can.'

They were standing in a convenient plantation of rhododendrons extending around two sides of the building. To approach the new wing they would have to break cover for forty yards, and cross a kitchen garden.

'Keep to the paths,' Cribb whispered. 'And watch that open window. I think there may be a lamp inside. This light's deceptive.'

They scudded as noiselessly as two large men could across the open area and halted at the grey wall itself, to the left of the open window. Cribb was correct; both of them glimpsed a flickering paraffin lamp as they passed within view of the room. And when Thackeray's agitated breathing subsided they could hear a low voice, too muffled for the words to be intelligible.

'I'll try to get closer,' Cribb breathed. 'May hear something useful. You move along the wall and look in the other windows. Careful, mind.'

Thackeray tiptoed away on his mission. He could never be sure at such times whether Cribb was giving him responsibility or making certain he was out of the way. His boot caught a flower-pot, and it toppled over and rolled through an arc on the gravel path. He stiffened against the wall, cursing his clumsiness.

For two minutes Thackeray waited, thoughts racing through his brain of action to take when he was discovered. The proper course was to hold them off as conspicuously as possible, giving Cribb a chance of flight. He looked around for a weapon. There was only the flower-pot. If the Ebony came in pursuit, no flower-pot would fell him. Thackeray decided to rely on a dash for the rhododendrons.

Nothing happened, so he edged forward again, calculating each footfall like a mountaineer. There was a window a few feet ahead. He stopped, straining to hear sounds within. Nothing. He leaned forward and moved his eye to the glass. The brim of his bowler made contact, and he jerked back with a small start.

The interior was sufficiently well-lit by the moon. Thackeray was looking into a spacious room, dominated by a platform-structure at the centre, a yard in height and at least twenty-four feet square: a full-scale boxing-ring with posts and ropes. To the left was an area equipped for gymnastics, with ropes suspended from the ceiling, two with rings. There were parallel and horizontal bars, a high bar and a trapeze. Scattered about the floor were Indian clubs and dumb-bells. He stayed at the window, making a mental inventory of every object within view. Somebody had provided handsomely for the Ebony's training.

Sergeant Cribb, after wincing at Thackeray's blunder with the flower-pot, waited fully three minutes before attempting to improve his position at the window. The speaking within continued. It was more monologue than conversation, the same teasingly subdued voice speaking at intervals and answered occasionally in monosyllables. Cribb crouched at sill-height and looked in.

The conversation became audible.

'... said he was probably a heavier man than you, and weight is important in fighting. Your physical construction is incomparable, of course, but crude weight is said to out-top muscle when there is enough of it. Are you feeling cooler now? This will surely keep you from getting muscle stiffness this time.'

To Cribb's surprise, the speaker was a woman. Her face was in shadow, but the voice and figure were young. She was standing beside a backless chaise-longue, talking as she applied liniment to the Ebony's dorsal muscles. He was lying quite naked, face downwards, his thighs and buttocks glistening darkly after massage.

'He was the best available,' she continued, pouring more of the liquid into her palm. The air at the window was heavy with its aroma. 'His record was in the champion class. Mostly straight knockdowns, too. It won't be easy to find another of his reputation. Your ribs must be sore. I'll dab them lightly.'

The Ebony's face was clearly visible from Cribb's position. The left eye was swollen, but he was otherwise unmarked. He was drowsy, and apparently indifferent to what his masseuse was saying as she stroked his skin. Once, though, when her flattery became obvious, his mouth twisted into a secret sneer.

'Next time I would like to watch you. I wouldn't be the first of my sex to attend a prize-fight. Plenty did in the past, when it was considered respectable. If I disguised myself I could pass as a youth, couldn't I?'

A meaningless grunt from the Ebony. His indifference was no discouragement to her. Using the jargon of sport with incredible naturalness, she talked on, her small hands probing the black

45

surface of his back to isolate and caress the individual bands of muscle.

'The difficulty, Sylvanus, is to find another antagonist for you. You aren't ready yet for the French or the Yankees, though you'll pole-axe them when the time comes. We took the others into the top class too soon. I shall not make that mistake with you. Besides –' she leaned forward to whisper something into his ear and a strand of hair that had become loose fell on his shoulder.

Outside, Cribb froze, feeling himself within her line of vision. But she straightened, and continued her work.

In those few seconds the sergeant was able to study her face. They were certainly a young woman's features, delicately fashioned, yet sharply defined. Dark, expressive eyes, elegant nose, cheeks flushed slightly, perhaps by the close heat of the Ebony's body. All the character, though, was in her mouth. It was a fraction wider than perfect proportion asked. The upper line almost arrogant in its precision. Below it a fuller, rounded lip. Sensuousness underlying vestal coldness.

'I may arrange for Edmund to bring a fighter down from the north,' she continued. 'He once told me of a group of fist-fighters in Manchester. You're not fighting any more farm-boys, I promise you. Would you lift your arms? If you fold them above your head I can work on your biceps.' She giggled slightly. 'You'll soon be my anointed one, Sylvanus. Hand-maidens did this for kings in ancient times.'

Cribb was studying the Ebony's face. Unmistakably it creased into an expression of contempt.

'These moths!' she said petulantly. 'The lamp draws them. Now that the rain has stopped it isn't possible to have a light near an open window. I'll draw the curtain. It's time Edmund unleashed the dogs.'

Cribb ducked, flattening himself to the wall. Thackeray, rejoining him from behind, stiffened to a halt.

There was the sound of heavy curtains being drawn.

Cribb gestured to Thackeray to move away.

The glint in the sergeant's eye was more than moonshine. 'I

don't know what you saw, Thackeray,' he whispered when they were sufficiently far away, 'but I've learned enough in the last ten minutes to get us both a quick promotion.'

Five

Brilliant in red and green it leaped and dived in the gusty air, a magnificent chequered kite, as large as its owners. In mid-afternoon a breath of wind had disturbed the trees, causing leaves to gleam momentarily silver in the sunlight. By tea-time you could call it a breeze and – splendid for kite-flying – it varied in force from one moment to the next. Now, in early evening, the kite, after being quiescent in a playroom for months, swooped and shivered above Richmond Green, while two small boys and Henry Jago struggled to control its flight.

Waiting there to intercept Lydia on her way to post her father's letters, he had found the kite impossible to resist. Clearly its elevation could be much improved with the help of strength and science. Soon the owners stood stiffly at a distance, occasionally playing out more cord. Jago, with his hands on the life-line, tugged and raced to achieve even greater height.

Lydia must have been watching for several minutes before he realized she was there.

His hand slipped down the cord in an automatic movement. The kite swooped downwards. Its protesting owners rushed to take control again.

'I thought you policemen discouraged kites,' she scolded as he came sheepishly to her.

'Kites? Oh yes. Very dangerous near roads, when they cause the horses to rear. Kites and hoops – the modern child *will* play with these dangerous toys. I'd have them banned myself.'

She smiled.

What a relief!

'Lydia, how can I apologize for your appalling disappointment yesterday evening? You did receive my letter in the afternoon? It was absolutely unavoidable. Short of disobeying orders, and losing my job, I couldn't possibly have come.'

'Yes, it *was* a disappoinment, Henry.'

Said so tolerantly! She either had an unshakeable affection for him, or she was unusually well-brought-up. Jago had known young ladies from good families who would have ended the acquaintanceship for less. Discarded him like last season's bonnet. And not without a torrent of abuse.

'I hope you were able to warn Stella in reasonable time. She was coming as chaperone, wasn't she?'

Lydia nodded. 'Papa drove round to tell her we could not go.'

The Colonel. If it was possible, his opinion of Jago would have sunk still lower. Bad enough that a young fellow decently educated should be so ill-advised as to join the blasted police force. But when he had the sheer impertinence to break a promise made to a lady – a serving officer's daughter – the bounder deserved cashiering at the very least.

'*She* was disappointed too, I expect.' Jago said this without excessive sympathy. Stella, Lydia's closest friend, invariably came as chaperone. She never said very much to him but her eyes spoke. 'You won't make much impression, Henry Jago. There are things I could tell her about you, and I probably will.'

'Yes,' answered Lydia. 'She was certainly looking forward to *The Corsican Brothers*. The Lyceum is her favourite theatre. Can you tell me what it was you had to do?'

Deuced awkward situation. She was being so charming about everything. He was bound to say something.

'I'm not officially permitted to say, but it *was* important work.' Stella, he was sure, would give *her* verdict on his activities. 'Detective work! He is no detective, Lydia, believe me. Why doesn't he wear his uniform when he takes you out, as any young subaltern does? He is ashamed, that's why. And not just ashamed of being merely a constable. I once passed him in Northumberland Avenue and saw his uniform. The seat of his trousers, my dear! It gleams like a mirror! He sits on a chair all day and pushes a pen. You've seen the ink-stains on his fingers, haven't you?'

'I hope it wasn't a policeman's smoking concert, anyway,' said Lydia, smiling.

'Not at all!' he said almost too vehemently, for a memory of his performance in the Fox had flashed through his mind. 'Quite the reverse. Strictly an evening on duty.' He looked about him and moved closer to her. 'I can at least say this, but in Heaven's name do not tell anyone – not even Stella – or I shall lose my job. Last night I was travelling in company with a group of men who may lead us to a most savage murderer. I was alone in a railway carriage with them.'

'Alone? But how dreadful, Henry! How did you prevent them from attacking you?'

'Ah. Disguise. In a manner of speaking. You see I was dressed as I am now, like any ordinary member of the public.'

'How clever. What happened?'

He opened his palms in a gesture of helplessness. 'I really cannot say. But this morning I was congratulated for the information I passed on.'

'Weren't you in terrible danger?'

He basked in her concern.

'Possibly. That is part of my job.'

'Then they shouldn't send you on such missions. I know you are an expert in boxing with the gloves, but what chance would you have against a gang of desperate ruffians? They could have recognized you and thrown you out of the moving train, or worse!'

Jago enjoyed himself thinking of the unspeakable injuries he had escaped. 'But here I am, Lydia, without a mark on me.' The moment he had said it, he realized how smug it sounded. 'Tell me how you are. What have you done today?'

They walked slowly across the Green, Lydia holding her father's letters ceremoniously, like an ambassador's credentials. They were her reason for walking in that direction and chancing to meet Henry Jago. It was only right that one should spare the servants a duty on occasions.

'Henry, do you think your prospects of advancement in the police are good?'

She looked up at him earnestly, blushing slightly at her own temerity, peachy cheeks touched by copper curls.

Jago cleared his throat nervously. 'I certainly hope so. There are many possibilities, but one has to prove oneself capable, as one does in any employment.'

'Papa was asking.'

'Really?' Was the Colonel actually taking him seriously?

'I didn't know quite what to say. I don't think he understands much about the police. He asked me whether you had good non-commissioned officers serving under you, as that could make a lot of difference to your platoon.'

'Oh.'

'I think he might be prepared to meet you again if you would like to leave your card. He realizes that he was rather abrupt last time. But when we first met at the West Surrey he gained the impression that you were a regimental man.'

'Yes, I remember.' Only his admiration for Lydia had prevented Jago from undeceiving the Colonel at once.

'If he knew you better he might allow you to call on us regularly. He is rather suspicious about my going out to post his letters, I fear. This one isn't the nearest posting-box to our house.'

Jago smiled appreciatively.

'Papa read your letter most carefully yesterday. He asked me a number of questions about you. Then he finished by saying that I should widen my circle of acquaintances. He has been introduced to the curate at St Martin's, a young gentleman recently from theological college, and we have been invited to call on him next Saturday.'

Jago blanched. 'I see.'

'Henry, I think you would find much in common with Papa, if you would call on us. You have told me yourself that the Force is organized like a military regiment. And then there is your sport.'

Jago tried to appear enthusiastic. 'Oh yes. He is interested in cricket, isn't he? I know a bit about Grace – W.G., you know, not the kind his curate friend specializes in.'

It was feeble humour, but both needed the chance to smile.

'He *does* enjoy cricket talk,' Lydia said. 'I think that is why he is interested in the curate. He scored a century for Cambridge.'

A pause.

'I could talk about boxing,' said Jago. 'Have you told him about my police championship victory?'

'No. Not yet.'

'My sergeant has just arranged for me to have intensive training in self-defence. Two hours a day. I shall be the most able-bodied bobby in London, Lydia!'

'Self-defence? Is that boxing?'

'Yes, but much more besides. I'm starting with a professor at Shoreditch School of Arms on Monday morning. I shall be instructed in the art of wrestling, as the Japanese practise it, and fist-fighting –'

'But what is it for, Henry?'

Altogether more buoyant now, Jago lifted his fists and mimed the classic stance of the pugilist.

'Self-defence. And fighting off jealous curates. I think I *shall* try again with your Papa, Lydia.'

She took his arm and they walked on to the posting-box.

In the records room at Great Scotland Yard, Constable Thackeray stretched his legs and turned his feet to examine the insteps of his best pair of regulation boots. The damp-line extended like a chalk mark all the way round. He doubted whether they would ever fully recover from their soaking the previous week in the Essex mud.

' "Beckett," ' read Sergeant Cribb aloud, ' "Matthew James. Born 1853. Five feet ten. Twelve stone two. Dark complexion. No permanent address. Last lodging in Bermondsey. Ex-seaman. Crown tattooed on right forearm. Serpent on left." Jago missed that. Let's see what the record is. "June 1873. Six months for housebreaking. March '76. Drunk and disorderly. One month. April '78. Loitering with intent to commit a felony. Fined £1." None of them violent crimes, you see, but he appeared to be the leader. Where's the last file?'

Thackeray handed it over.

'"Foster, David. Born 1860. Five foot six. Ten stone." Beautiful copper-plate, this. Only one entry. Drunk and disorderly again. I can believe that too, after Friday evening in that Rainham tap-room.' He tossed the file back to Thackeray. 'That's the four with records, then. Three tough coves and one young 'un. Capital work of Jago's to pick 'em out.'

'I think he knows these records like the coins in his pocket, Sarge. That could well be his own handwriting you admired. Is there anything on Meanix himself?'

'Not here,' Cribb answered. 'So many charges were brought a few years back for prize-fighting that the records were never centralized. You'll find a better account of him in *Fistiana* than anywhere else. No, it's the bunch who followed him that interests me.'

'Was anything said, Sarge?'

'Plenty. Young Jago's less dumb than he looks. Gave me enough to hook in most of his fellow-travellers on suspicion if I needed to.'

'You won't, then?'

'Wouldn't help at present. I need something more decisive and I think I know where to find it. Someone's got to lead me to the killer. I'm leaving every possibility open at present. Things will happen in the next week. Almost sure to.'

'Why, Sarge?'

'The gang. If Meanix had done his job they stood to make a mint.'

Thackeray was dubious. 'I don't see how that was possible, Sarge. The odds were heavily in his favour from the start.'

Cribb sometimes despaired of his assistant.

'Side-bets, Constable, side-bets. First knockdown, first blood, length of contest. Meanix was hired to engineer that fight to order, round by round. And he would have done, with different opposition. They expected a muscle-bound ploughman in the village-idiot class. The Ebony was quite a different kettle.'

'So they lost heavily,' concluded Thackeray.

'Not so heavily. There was time to hedge their bets when they saw the Ebony's form. But they gained nothing. And with Meanix a spent force they've got to hire a new punching-machine. From what Jago heard they'd like to take over the Ebony.'

'What will happen to Meanix?'

The edges of Cribb's mouth creased into a smile.

'Thackeray, I know what you're thinking. The Ox to the slaughterhouse, eh? You could be right, too. I think they'll put him to grass, though.'

'Could our headless fighter be another one who disappointed them?' ventured Thackeray.

'I think not.' Cribb flexed an arm, stood up, and walked to the window, to look across Great Scotland Yard. 'Dispatching a pug in London ain't that easy, even if you top him first. Questions get asked. People miss him in the pubs and training gyms. It's a week now since I fished him out of the river.'

Thackeray stroked his beard sagely. 'We've enough listeners in the pubs to have picked something up by now.'

'Exactly. London turns up nothing, so where do we look?'

'Essex or Kent, I suppose, Sarge. But don't the same things apply? If he was a provincial man, the chances of someone local missing him would be far greater than in London, I'd say.'

'Certainly,' said Cribb. 'What if he were imported, though, and kept in a place like Radstock Hall? D'you suppose the Ebony is a Rainham man? Who do you think would ask questions if he disappeared tomorrow and wasn't seen again? I heard that woman talk of other fighters, men who were pushed too soon into the top class. Suppose one of them was badly beaten, killed even, by Meanix, or one of the London pugs.'

Thackeray saw the implication.

'Nobody would ask questions, because nobody knows how many fighters are kept at Radstock Hall, or where they come from.'

Cribb scarcely heard the remark. He was in a strangely restive mood. He turned from the window.

'Sunshine,' he informed Thackeray. 'Rare enough in London. Let's get out in it.'

The constable needed no second bidding. Scotland Yard's stained oak and dark leather depressed him too. He almost envied young Jago's two hours that morning with his professor in the art of self-defence. Cribb seemed drawn to the river as though it would yield the secret of the headless pugs if he visited it enough. Reaching the Embankment, he set out purposefully towards Waterloo Bridge, at a pace too athletic for Thackeray's comfort on a summer morning. Strolling nannies heard the brisk approach of boots and moved their perambulators aside. Children in sailor suits looked up from games of ducks and drakes at the water's edge.

'Fine respect we have for human life,' Cribb said with scorn. 'What is it – ten years since the Embankment opened? What happens if a nipper chases a hoop over the edge? Look down here. See the lion's mouth bosses in the granite? They were linked with chains in the designs. Here we are in 1880 with not a chain in place. If you fell in at any point between Westminster Bridge and Blackfriars you couldn't find a chain, nor a rope nor a boom for a handhold in the length of the Embankment. No wonder they make a business out of collecting bodies in King's Reach.'

Thankful for a pause, Thackeray made it clear from his stance that he planned a few moments' study of the river traffic. A Thames Company paddle steamer sounded a scape-pipe warning to a coal barge on the South Bank side.

'Devil's own vessels, paddle boats,' commented Cribb, warming to his theme. 'As cock-eyed a system of navigation as you'll find. Captain passes on his orders from the bridge through deaf and dumb finger talk to a rating, and he tries to make the engineer understand. More often than not results in chaos. Next time you visit the boat race take a close look at the flotilla that follows it up. For my money those steam-boat skippers provide better sport than the oarsmen out front. I've seen a solid wall of eight steamers jammed sponson to sponson and crammed with old Blues go full bat at a buttress of Hammersmith Bridge. You couldn't drag me aboard. I'd sooner sweat it out in one of the eights.'

Thackeray cast an analytical eye down Cribb's gaunt frame.

'You ain't the rowing build, Sarge. Nor am I come to that, though I might have been twenty or thirty years back. Now Constable Jago *would* look well in a boat. He must have done some rowing at school, I dare say, being a public school man. I still can't understand what made him join the Force, he being such a one for manly exercises. Oxford or Cambridge was the proper place for a young fellow of his breeding.'

Cribb made a snorting sound deep in his nostrils.

'He'll get his share of exercise soon enough.'

Thackeray enjoyed the joke.

'You think the professor will make him sweat a bit, Sarge?'

'I hope so. He needs to be fit to take up knuckle-fighting.'

Silence, while Thackeray wrestled with the significance of what Cribb had said. The sergeant's callous streak was not new to him; indeed, he had suffered personally from it many times. But victimization of a hardened veteran was one thing: sentencing young Jago to certain butchery was brutal beyond belief. He rounded on Cribb.

'You can't make him do that! He's got no experience. He'll be torn to ribbons.'

Cribb said nothing, seeming more interested in a passing skiff than Thackeray's indignation.

'We can't use Jago, Sarge. You saw what happened to Meanix, and he was a seasoned knuckle-fighter. Young Jago doesn't fight their way. Queensberry Rules don't permit wrestling and spiking and kidney-punching. It's like matching a farm-bird with a fighting cock.'

'He's game,' said Cribb airily. 'And I've fixed lessons for him to learn some of the tricks.'

'He'll need more than a few tricks,' Thackeray commented bitterly. 'I don't think you should ask a man to do such a thing. He'd feel obliged to say yes, having been moved to your Division to help you. But he's no knuckle-fighter –'

'Police champion,' interjected Cribb.

'Yes, but at glove-fighting, and that's as different as milk is from brandy. What good can it do to have a promising young bobby beaten to pulp in a prize-ring?'

'I guessed you might take it amiss, Thackeray. The plain fact is that I need to get an informant inside Radstock Hall. Listening at windows has its uses, but it ain't the most thoroughgoing method of inquiry, now is it? I've seen and heard enough this twenty-four hours to make me think we could be uncovering a very ugly set of crimes – as vicious as anything I've come across. Now there's things to be learned at Radstock Hall, I'm sure, but they'll take time and smart detective work. I need someone there who's in their confidence. I want to know all about those fighters who failed, and I want the place examined – not obviously, but methodically over several days. I'm not asking Jago to dig for severed heads. I just want to know what's happening there, and what's been happening since the Vibarts moved in. Jago's no mean performer with his fists. He ought to give a fair impersonation of a promising pug. He may not need to fight in earnest at all. But if the situation arises, I know when to intervene.'

Thackeray was far from convinced.

'I don't like this at all, Sarge. He's strong and able, is young Jago, but he's not one quarter as sharp as you are. It's not easy passing yourself off as something you ain't, even if you take on a false name –'

'He won't,' said Cribb.

'No false name, Sarge? But they could identify him as one of the Force, and then there's nothing to prevent them killing him, if they're the bunch we think they are.'

The sergeant shook his head emphatically. 'I want this simple. We'll leave play-acting out of it. If a false name confused anyone it'd be Jago himself. They've no way of checking if he's a Scotland Yard man – he's strictly on clerical duties, as you know, so his name's not quite a household word. Don't worry. We'll let slip enough genuine information about Jago to satisfy 'em. They won't be expecting members of the Force to masquerade as fistfighters, anyway. That's not the way we're supposed to work.'

'He'll need to keep his wits about him,' said Thackeray dubiously.

'He's no use in Criminal Investigation if he can't,' commented Cribb.

Thackeray cast about for another means of penetrating the sergeant's indifference.

'How will he get into Radstock Hall, then?'

'Shouldn't be any trouble,' said Cribb. 'He's known in his gym at the Anchor. Once the word gets round that he's game to fight with the raw 'uns there should be offers enough. Anyone can see he's primely built for pugilism and there aren't that many fist-fighters about. The Essex bunch are professionals: they wouldn't build a gym like the one you saw if they weren't investing heavily in the game. When Jago's on the market they'll be interested, believe me.'

When Cribb put it that way, Thackeray found it all too plausible.

'But they'll want him to live in Radstock Hall, like the Ebony.'

'Without a doubt.'

Thackeray played his final card.

'What about his young lady, then?'

'His what?' So Cribb had actually overlooked something.

'The young lady at Richmond. A high-spirited young woman from Jago's account of her. But he's very sweet on her. A redhead, I think he said, and deuced attractive. How do you muzzle one of the fair sex?'

Cribb walked in silence, plainly ruffled.

'I'm damned if I know,' he admitted at last.

Six

'You'll be waiting for someone to pick you up, I dare say, sir.'

Henry Jago nodded. He had been sipping a half-pint of beer for forty-five minutes already. Since he was the only customer in the Fox and Grapes that afternoon, and his portmanteau stood inside the door, he could hardly deny the landlord's conclusion.

'Going up to the 'All, are you?' The landlord was drying freshly washed tankards and wanted to talk as he worked. It was a difficult situation.

'Radstock Hall,' Jago admitted.

'Ah, Mr Vibart should be coming for you with the trap, then. You'll 'ave a pleasant drive through the lanes this fine afternoon. Makes a change, don't it? Been there before, 'ave you?'

'No, I can't say I have.'

'Ah.' This was uttered with great emphasis.

Three tankards later the landlord began again.

'I thought when you came in off the train, I thought here's a lissome lad. If he's going anywhere it's up to Vibart's place. Most of the parties that go up to the 'All stop off 'ere, you see. Big lads, all of 'em. You'll 'ave a good show of muscle round the epaulettes yourself, I can see. Funny, you know. What gives you scrappers away ain't so much your build, or what you say. It's what you drink – or rather what you don't. I always say that a classy scrapper knows what's good for 'im. Beer and bare-fists don't mix, do they? If a pug can't keep 'is elbow down there ain't much future for 'im.'

There was no point in playing dumb, Jago decided. He should have recognized the landlord before as the referee at the fight between Meanix and the Ebony.

'You sound a connoisseur, landlord.'

The innkeeper came beaming round the counter.

'I think that's a fair description, sir. There ain't many I've not seen in the last twenty or thirty years – swells, Jews, Yankees, gippos – some capital fighters, I can tell you. In the palmy days, when the beaks winked at a fist-fight, I 'ad matches every week out the back 'ere, in my yard. And we drew the gentry like yourself down from London – Lords, Judges, Parliamentarians. Get a man like Mace in the magic circle and there wasn't no limit to the class of spectator, royalty included.'

Jago saw possibilities in this conversation.

'It's quite another story now, though.'

The landlord needed little prompting. 'True, very true. The rough element – the sharp boys – spoilt it for the rest. If it weren't for them money-grabbing fellows cutting rough we'd 'ave open fist-fighting today. I might say that I do admire Mrs Vibart for what she's doing for the sport.'

'*Mrs* Vibart?'

'Yes. Ah, you won't 'ave met the lady yet. Your dealings will 'ave been with Edmund, I dare say. She's the guvnor up at Radstock 'All, though, believe me. Never seen a public fist-fight in 'er life, but knows the London prize-ring rules better than our vicar knows 'is Ten Commandments. If you're invited to join the Radstock 'All bunch it's at Mrs Vibart's invitation, I can tell you.'

Jago had his instructions from Cribb to discover more about the occupants of Radstock Hall. This, if it could be believed, was sensational information.

'It's most irregular, a woman taking an active interest in a man's sport.'

'Most irregular woman altogether,' commented the landlord. 'She's got an eye for a fighter all right. You may 'ave 'eard of the Ebony. Mrs Vibart's pet 'e 'is. Now if you want to see a pair of dukes attending to a man's complexion watch that Negro fight. As pretty a mover as you'll see, and weighty with it. I wouldn't spar with 'im unless 'e's wearing mittens, and that's sound advice.'

Sound, but superfluous. Cribb and Thackeray had both made the same point earlier that day.

The landlord wiped a window with his cloth.

'Don't see no sign of 'im. If 'e's stopped off at the church there's no telling when the old bugger'll show up.'

'Oh,' said Jago, with interest. 'He's a religious man, is he?'

'Religious?' The connection seemed to escape the landlord. 'Who, Vibart? You don't know much about your friends at Radstock 'All do you? Vibart's the organist at the church 'ere and if you think that makes 'im religious you ought to 'ear the language 'e uses when he 'its a wrong note, which is three or four times a service. There's mothers in Rainham that's stopped their boys from singing in the choir because of it. Vibart enjoys 'imself though, and the vicar can't find nobody else.' He shook his head. 'You might be better off making your own way there. I could send your luggage on later. You don't ride a bicycle, do you? You could borrow mine. Beautiful machine. India-rubber tyres. Take you 'alf the time.'

Jago appreciated the generosity. The gleaming penny-farthing in the passage had caught his eye earlier.

'Thanks, but I'm a duffer at balancing.'

The landlord clapped a hand to his forehead.

'Blimey, of course you are! You're the lad that fell flat on 'is face in 'ere the other night. I thought there was something about you.' He began to shake with laughter. 'Well don't make an 'abit of it, lad, or Mrs Vibart'll feed you to the Ebony for breakfast!'

To Jago's relief the merriment was cut short by the entry of Edmund Vibart.

'Henry Jago? Sorry I'm late. We cast a shoe on the first attempt and I had to go back and change the bloody horse. That's your luggage, is it? Would you put it aboard, landlord? Then you can draw me a large beer. Welcome to Rainham, Jago! Hades apart, you won't find a more God-forsaken hole than this.'

Jago smiled, and inwardly recoiled. Vibart exuded sweat and self-importance. His clothes, broad check suit, silk shirt, crimson cravat and matching kerchief, jarred even on a sportsman's sensibility.

'You're a sizeable fellow, aren't you? I shan't pick a bloody fight with you – not until we've trimmed you down a bit, eh? What's your weight?'

'Around twelve stone, I believe.'

Jago under scrutiny felt as he imagined a bullock feels in a beef-stock sale.

'Not a bad weight. Not bad at all. You can reckon to lose a stone in the first two weeks of serious training. That's if we take you on, of course. Stand up. Let's see your height.'

'Whatever happens, co-operate,' Cribb had ordered Jago. That was going to call for extraordinary self-discipline. He got to his feet, trying to think of it as a duty sergeant's inspection. Vibart's head came close, at the level of Jago's necktie. Macassar, cheap and pungent, invaded his nostrils.

'Good height, too. Six foot, I'd say, give half an inch either way.'

Jago fully expected a sweaty hand to force his lips apart for a dental inspection. Instead Vibart took a step back, gave one more approving look at his build, and turned to the ale waiting on the table. In seconds it was gone. Then without another glance at Jago he planted a deerstalker on his head and marched to the door.

'No time for another, landlord. We must get back. I may be in again in a day or two. Mrs Vibart has plans for another set-to, you understand.'

'Very good, sir.'

As Jago followed, the landlord came with him to the door.

'Don't mind 'im, young 'un,' he murmured. 'But watch out for the lady.'

Driving through the lanes was as pleasant as the innkeeper predicted. The surface was badly rutted in places, but it was a well-sprung dog-cart. Jago looked out across vegetable crops intersected by low hedges, and thought of Cribb and Thackeray tramping by night across the same fields. There were compensations in being a junior constable.

Having made his assessment of Jago's physique, Vibart was not much interested in conversation.

'Is it far?' Jago ventured.

'Far enough.'

'Not really a walking proposition, then?'

'If it was,' Vibart snapped, 'I wouldn't be acting as bloody cabby, would I?'

They passed a field where a ploughman was at work patterning the scene with furrows, pursued by flocks of scavenging birds. His face turned to watch the passing trap, but there was no wave of recognition.

'Do you have many servants at the Hall?' Jago asked.

'One cook, one maid, one gardener. Germans.'

'Ah, that's enough I expect. Does your wife –'

'My *what*?' Vibart turned a scandalized face towards Jago.

'Mrs Vibart. Isn't she – I'm most terribly sorry if I've jumped to a wrong conclusion,' said Jago, rather pleased at his guile. 'I just assumed –'

'She's my sister-in-law. Percy, my older brother, married her a year ago. Died of heart failure last Christmas. He was close to twenty years older than her. She inherited the entire bloody estate. I have my rooms there and help with the sporting arrangements. A woman can't do business with the Fancy, you see, so I act as agent. Blasted messenger-boy and cabman, that's my function.'

Vibart was plainly too obsessed with the indignity of his personal position to volunteer more information. They drove on in silence.

The approach to Radstock Hall was through a copse, and the air was distinctly cooler in the shade. A pair of wrought-iron gates barred the entrance to the grounds.

'Hold the reins while I unlock,' ordered Vibart. 'Don't be alarmed if you hear barking. We keep two dogs in the lodge.'

The din from inside the small building adjacent to the entrance was intimidating when Vibart touched the gates.

'Ferocious blasted animals,' he commented when he rejoined Jago. 'They eat more steak than you could in a week and they'd still go for your throat if you met them off the chain. I'd have them shot myself, but she's attached to them.'

The front aspect of the Hall was grand in its way, Jago decided as they drove towards it, but certainly inferior to Chapeldurham, ancestral home of the Jagos. The amber glow of brickwork in the afternoon sun was pleasing, but ivy had taken a grip, and obscured much of the builder's handiwork. It was too symmetrical, anyway, with twin gables flanking the turreted entrance porch, and precisely positioned casements. And the height of the chimney stacks was unsightly, if not dangerous.

Vibart's pull at the bell-rope was answered by the maid, a humourless woman in her fifties.

'The mistress will take tea with you in the sun-lounge when you have unpacked,' she told Jago in a heavy accent as she led him through a panelled entrance hall to the stairs. Vibart, his mission completed, had slipped away without a word.

'I hope you find it satisfactory, sir.'

It was a small, comfortably furnished bedroom at the rear of the house, with brass bedstead, commode, wardrobe and arm-chair. All it lacked was ornaments, the sentimental knick-knackery that gave a room personality. Jago lifted his portman-teau on to the bed, took out Blondin and placed him reverently in the centre of the mantelshelf. Then he removed his jacket, lifted the water-jug from its basin on the commode and began to wash his hands, whistling. From the window he could see the flat roof of the new grey-brick wing Cribb had described. That would be the gym. He looked forward to using it.

Fifteen minutes later Jago edged open the door of the sun-lounge.

'Please come in, Mr Jago. You must be ready for tea.'

A low-pitched voice for a woman, authoritative but not un-feminine.

'Over here. One has to force one's way through the greenery, I know, but I like to take tea here in the summer.'

She was seated in a bamboo chair, almost obscured by a large semi-tropical shrub. Jago saw at once that Cribb's description of 'a deuced fine-looking woman' was gross understatement. Mrs Vibart was magnetic; simultaneously demure and alluring.

She put forward a slender hand.

'Do be seated. I shall pour the tea. As a man in training you do without milk, I expect?'

'If you please.' Jago was not particularly concerned about the contents of his tea-cup. He settled opposite her in a cane-chair, marvelling that so elegant a creature could interest herself in the brutalities of the ring.

'Edmund was late, I understand. He is usually reliable. I expect he explained that he is the brother of my late husband. He is less intelligent than Percy was, and has none of his charm. You will doubtless have formed your opinion, however. A scone?'

'Thank you.' Jago's social training took over. 'You have given me a most comfortable room, Mrs Vibart.'

She smiled. The parting of her lips caused Jago's knee to jerk involuntarily. He re-crossed his legs.

'It is very small, but I think you should be comfortable there. If you decide to remain with us you will not need to spend much time in your room. I have a well-equipped gymnasium – better, I believe, than the one you are used to, a billiard-room and several lounges. Now, Mr Jago –' she pushed the bamboo table and tea-tray aside '– you are interested in fighting professionally, I believe.'

'That is so.' Jago hastily regrouped his thoughts.

'And you have some experience of amateur boxing?' She used the term as though it were foreign to her conversation.

'Yes, in a limited way. For two years.'

'Have you won any championships?'

'I did not bother to enter,' lied Jago. 'Until recently, my only interest was in an occasional bout with a skilful opponent. I have sometimes beaten quite reputable amateurs.'

A pause. It was going almost exactly as Cribb had rehearsed it the day before. Except that Cribb lacked the power to distract.

'Mr Jago. You are patently a gentleman. Where were you educated?'

'Privately, by tutor.' Public school records would be easy to check.

'And your university?'

This at least would be true. 'I had a difference with my father and decided to forgo university.'

'Really? That was rather perverse.' The smile again. 'What did you do then?'

'I tried to make my way in the legal profession, not too successfully.'

'I think I know the rest,' said Mrs Vibart. 'You met a young woman who lives in Richmond and you hope to marry her, but your present financial position is such that you could not presume to discuss it with her father.'

This much Cribb had agreed could be let slip to Jago's contact at the Anchor. Yet hearing the details repeated so faithfully by Mrs Vibart alerted Jago to the seriousness of his position. Every part of his story would be checked.

'And so you want to make money, large amounts of money, from your skill as a fighter.'

'If I can.'

'We shall see. If you have the ability the prizes are considerable. What will you say if your prospective father-in-law asks where your fortune came from?'

It was a question Cribb had not anticipated. Jago thought of Colonel Boltover.

'My feeling is that he would be sufficiently impressed by the money not to inquire where it came from, but if he discovered the truth I doubt whether it would make much difference. He is a sportsman.' Correct in its way, although Boltover's enthusiasm for Lord's was unlikely ever to extend to secret prizerings in Essex fields.

'I hope you are right. I should not want your . . . new interests here to lead to an estrangement between you and the young lady.' Mrs Vibart spoke with a strange emphasis. Jago felt the colour begin to rise to his cheeks. Blushing had always been his problem, a grave handicap to a plain-clothes man. 'Well, Mr Jago,' she said, 'I must show you my gymnasium.'

It was of small significance, but Jago was fascinated by Mrs Vibart's poise. Throughout their conversation she had sat forward on her chair, as upright as a governess, emphasizing the cut of her velvet bodice. And now she rose with scarcely any tilt of her body. As an athlete Jago marvelled at such control. She had, in effect, performed a standard gymnastic exercise which he often practised. Even allowing for her slight build and the probable support of a corset, she could not have risen so elegantly without considerable power in her thighs. Jago blushed again.

She led him through a billiard-room, superbly equipped,

where her brother-in-law was practising shots. He did not look up as they passed.

'Here it is,' she said, opening a baize-covered door. 'Mind that you say it impresses you, Mr Jago, because I am very proud of my gymnasium.'

No need for deception. He had never seen a hall so comprehensively equipped. Each activity had its own section of apparatus: vaulting standards and boxes, ropes and bars for climbing; dumb-bells and weights; punching-bags; and, at the far end, a full-sized ring.

'Unbelievable!'

'So everyone says.'

'How many fighters are you training here?' Jago asked.

'At present, only one. You will meet him later.'

'Was all this built for him?'

She laughed. 'Oh no. There were others. They left us, though. It is not easy to stay long in the top class, as you will find.'

'Who were they?'

'Oh they came from the Midlands. You wouldn't have known them.'

'And did they win their fights?'

'Mostly. I should now like to see you exercise, Mr Jago, if you are not too tired. There is a dressing-room over there, and you will find drawers and pumps to fit you. I shall wait here.'

Mrs Vibart's request was made almost whimsically. But when Jago entered the dressing-room he realized that his appearance in the gym was prescribed some time before. The accommodation was spacious enough for a football team, but only two cubicles were labelled. The first, in excellent copper-plate, read 'Sylvanus Morgan' and the second 'Henry Jago'. Inside were freshly laundered white boxing-drawers with a black sash. He changed, and found them a sound fit. Under the bench were two pairs of gym-shoes. The first he tried were right.

Bodily display was not usually embarrassing to Jago; stripping for the gym had become daily routine. This afternoon it was an ordeal. As he entered the vastness of the gym, conscious that everything he wore was owned and chosen by Mrs Vibart, he felt as naked as Adam.

'Come over here, Henry Jago,' the Christian name spoken with emphasis, as though to impress on him that he could not preserve formalities now; although when he really considered it, 'Mr Jago' did seem inappropriate in white drawers. 'Edmund is right. You have an excellent physique. Don't stand over there. I want to examine you.'

Jago advanced to be examined.

For perhaps fifteen seconds Mrs Vibart's eyes travelled over his body.

'A good pectoral development and strong biceps. That suggests work with dumb-bells or bar-bells. Your neck is quite strong-looking too, isn't it? The legs could improve with some work, I think. How are your abdominal muscles? May I feel?'

She pushed her hand firmly into his diaphragm.

'That, Henry Jago, seems your weakest point. Flex it, please.' With the side of her hand she prodded the area below Jago's ribs. 'Yes, we can strengthen you there. You wouldn't last long in a fist-fight in your present condition. Have you ever used a rowing-machine?'

'I did some rowing ... years ago,' said Jago. The words 'at school' had almost slipped out.

'Several years, I should think,' said Mrs Vibart, smiling. 'You are an admirer of Blondin, my maid tells me. His abdominal muscles are uncommonly powerful, or he would never retain his balance. I don't advise you to attempt to cross Niagara Falls for the present.'

Jago smiled, remembering his exhibition in the Fox.

'Let me see your back.'

Jago turned.

'Flex the arms please, and hold that position.'

'You've found another one then, Isabel. And quite a handsome show of flesh, eh?' A man's voice, suddenly close to where Mrs Vibart was standing.

'Robert? You've come back early. Turn round, Mr Jago,

and meet Mr D'Estin. Robert is a family friend, and I hope that he will agree to train you.'

Jago obeyed.

He was eye to eye with one of the most powerful men he had encountered. If Mrs Vibart set her physical standards by Robert D'Estin, Jago could see why his own physique had not been passed as perfect. Yet there was nothing gorilla-like about him; he was uniformly well-proportioned, and good-looking. The face intelligent and clear-skinned, the moustache neatly barbered. He held a silver-topped cane.

'Glad to meet you, Jago.'

A handshake.

The sensation was so unexpected that Jago could not disguise his shock. The hand that gripped his had three fingers missing.

'Accident with a duck-gun,' D'Estin explained. 'Four-bore. A good gun too, from Bond Street. The barrel blew up. Improperly cleaned, you see, so I've got this to remind me. The bastard that neglected his job has his own souvenir of the occasion. I saw to that.'

Jago was sometimes grateful for a limited imagination. Violence allied to such power was appalling to contemplate.

'Well, Mr Jago,' said Mrs Vibart, formal again in D'Estin's presence, 'I would like to ask you to use my gymnasium. I am sure that Robert would like to see you exercise.'

It was a relief to turn to activity, and less of an ordeal now that it was not for an audience of one. He picked up a skipping-rope and loosened his muscles with two minutes' work. Then the five-pound dumb-bells, curling them slowly up from arm's length twenty times: and then twenty pushes upwards from the shoulders. After this he jumped for the rings suspended from a beam, and swung his body upside down, pulled his shoulders to ring-level and then righted himself slowly. These were not exhibition pieces, but he preferred to perform efficiently and conscientiously.

'Now the saw-dust bag,' called D'Estin. 'Let's see your fists working.'

Jago moved over to where a large sack was suspended, and

began working at it, finding a rhythm in his punching, and weaving and feinting as he had learned in the Anchor gym.

'Good. You move well,' said D'Estin finally. 'Let's see your hands.'

Jago walked over and opened his palms.

'The knuckles, man.'

He turned them over. They were red from the roughness of the hessian.

'Tender, are they?' D'Estin asked, without much sympathy in the expression. 'They want pickling. When do we start, Isabel? Can we get these delicate dukes in vinegar tonight? The sooner the better.'

'What do you think, Mr Jago?' she asked, smiling again. 'Are you still game for a fist-fighting career?'

'If you'll take me on.' He was beginning to enjoy the prospect.

'Very good. I don't have to tell you that shedding the gloves has its dangers for a fighter, outside the ring as well as in. A fist-fighter blatantly breaks the law; if you are arrested at a prize-fight you can offer no defence. The penalties will be heavy. There are compensations, however. We shall keep you in food and lodging, and you will be paid five shillings a day while you are in training. My commission on your fights is fifty per cent of your earnings. Is that acceptable?'

'Entirely.' It was rather better than he was getting at Scotland Yard.

'Excellent. I think we can spare him the vinegar-treatment until tomorrow, Robert, but he will need physicking, of course.'

'Physicking?' queried Jago.

'The first step in getting a man fit, my friend,' D'Estin explained. 'A strong emetic, and then purging with Glauber's salts. A week of dosing should get your stomach clear.'

Seven

Two communications of great significance were delivered to Sergeant Cribb on the following Friday.

The first was a telegraph message:

BIRMINGHAM CONSTABULARY, JULY 20TH

RE YOUR INQUIRY JULY 19 CONFIRM THAT MISSING PERSONS REGISTER INCLUDES TWO BRICKMAKERS STOP DANIEL IVES 47 HEIGHT 5 FEET 2 INCHES WEIGHT 9 STONE HAIR BROWN AND THIN STOP LEFT HOME DECEMBER LAST STOP THREE CONVICTIONS DRUNKENESS STOP THOMAS QUINTON 38 HEIGHT 5 FEET 9 INCHES WEIGHT 12 STONE HAIR REDDISH BROWN STOP DESERTED WIFE APRIL THIS YEAR STOP TWO CONVICTIONS COMMON ASSAULT STOP AWAIT YOUR FURTHER ADVICE.

The second was post-marked Rainham, Essex:

Radstock Hall,
19th July, 1880

Second Report of Investigation presently being conducted at Radstock Hall, Rainham by 325, Jago, Henry Fortescue, Police Constable attached to M Division

Further to my Report of 16th Inst. I have the honour to submit the following account of subsequent developments.

July 17th. I passed this day in abject discomfort, the direct consequence of the two ounces of Glauber's salts administered to me the evening before. I was awakened at six by D'Estin, who ordered me to strip and then advanced on me with horsehair gloves and rubbed my flesh into an inflamed state. The cold bath that followed cooled me somewhat before the rubbing began afresh. Then a two-mile walk outside the grounds, which in other circumstances I should have enjoyed. On this occasion it was with some relief that I returned to the Hall. Breakfast followed, consisting of a broiled cutlet of mutton, stale bread and strong tea. D'Estin then took me in hand again, the morning's programme consisting of alternating showers and massage. After the mid-day meal, for which I was served roast beef, stale bread, a mealy potato and a small portion of greens, I was allowed to move about gently until nature had been complied with, and then to the gymnasium. Much bar-bell work and some sparring with the sack, all under D'Estin's direction. Then more rubbing, another shower, and a slow walk through the grounds. Two lightly boiled eggs and dry toast for tea.

I did not see Mrs Vibart at all during the day. The Ebony I met briefly at tea, but found him uncommunicative. He was not present at all during the evening when I played billiards with D'Estin. I retired soon after eleven, but no sooner had I drawn on my nightshirt than the water-jug commenced to vibrate and rattle so noisily that I began to suspect a poltergeist was at work. When I raised the jug from its position on the commode I found that I could hear the real origin of the vibrations. From somewhere in my wing of the house came the strains of organ-music, some fugue of Bach so inexpertly rendered that I at once set the water-jug down, where its rattling drowned the sound for the next forty minutes. Vibart, it seems, has a chamber organ in his bedroom, and is accustomed to practise before retiring. Others in the house may find his playing conducive to sleep; I lay awake long after he had stopped.

Wednesday's programme was identical to Tuesday's, even to the composition of the meals. But after tea I was asked to report to Mrs Vibart in the drawing-room, Edmund Vibart also being present. Mrs Vibart inquired about my progress, and seemed pleased enough with the answers I gave. She then informed me that a 'test' was being arranged for me this coming Saturday. Edmund has contracted for a local man to spar with me in the yard of the Fox and Grapes, commencing seven o'clock. It is not to be an articled contest, but a hat will be passed round after, and the contributions shared between us. I am to be attended by Vibart (bottle-holder) and D'Estin (second). My instructions are to let the fight run for ten rounds and then to try to finish it. My opponent is said to be well-made and strong, but not so spry as I am.

Mrs Vibart asked whether I had any questions regarding the fight, and I thought it timely to inquire whether I should be allowed to spar with Morgan (the Ebony) to sharpen my preparation. This elicited a significant response, both Mrs Vibart and her brother-in-law spiritedly resisting the suggestion. When the time was right, they informed me, I should go into the ring with Morgan, but I should on no account face him before. Since sparring was all that I suggested, the agitation in their refusal surprised me somewhat.

In the evening, after billiards, D'Estin applied lemon-juice to my face to toughen the skin, and pickled my hands as usual. Then to my disquiet he insisted that I took a Seidlitz powder before retiring, a quite superfluous inducement to my system. The consequences of this, and an hour or more of the 'Old Hundredth' abominably rendered by Vibart on his organ, combined to reduce my sleep to a minimum.

Today, Thursday, has followed the same sequence of events, although my activity has tended to be more intestinal than gymnastic. I hope, if I have recovered somewhat by this afternoon, to take a training walk to Rainham, and there to post this report. I shall, if asked, tell D'Estin that it is a letter to my future fiancee. I have been quite unable so far to induce him to discuss the pugilists who trained previously at the Hall. I have not forgotten your instruction to begin a systematic search of the building, but the opportunity has not arisen, for they rarely leave me alone. I searched my room for possible evidence of an earlier occupant, but found nothing.

I shall continue to send reports when I can. It should be possible, if you wish, to pass a message to me at the bout on Saturday evening.

In some haste,

Your obedient servant,

H. Jago, P.C.

'I feel for him, reading that,' said Thackeray, returning the report to Cribb. 'It almost goes beyond the call of duty, suffering of that kind. I'm not sure I could face it.'

'After two ounces of Glauber's salts and a Seidlitz powder you'd answer the call, Thackeray, depend upon it,' Cribb assured him breezily. 'You saw the telegraph. We're making progress at last. If Jago hadn't got the tip about the Midlands and sent it in his first report we'd still be looking for our pug.'

'You think this Quinton may be the headless man, Sarge?'

'Think? I'm sure of it. Everything's right – age, size, colour of hair – even the convictions. Common assault has often simply meant a prize-fight before now. I've got the widow coming down to look at the clothes. With luck, she'll identify them.'

'What made you pick Birmingham, Sarge?'

'I didn't particularly. All the Forces up there got my inquiry: Leicester, Northampton, all of them. Brum was likeliest to turn something up, though, once we had the word to try the Midlands. Several of the bare-fisted division live there, or in Wolverhampton. Usually they fight with gloves these days, but some make exceptions.'

'Charlie Mitchell?' suggested Thackeray.

'You're becoming quite a Corinthian, Constable. Would you care to see a fight on Saturday?'

'Seven o'clock, Fox and Grapes? I wouldn't miss it, Sarge.'

'Nor I. We'll need to look a trifle different from last time, though. Can't be known as regulars. Tweeds and deerstalker for me. You're easy. You just shave off your beard.'

Thackeray started back in horror.

'My beard, Sarge?'

'Yes. Soon grows again. Jago's suffering in the cause of duty. Must show solidarity, eh, Constable?'

It was disturbingly unreal, wholly unlike the setting for Meanix and the Ebony. The declining sun, impossibly red, made a woodcarving of the yard and its occupants. Probing light and deep shadow chiselled trivial details, door-frames, eaves, coach-wheels into sharp significance. Old men seated at tables with tankards had their nutcracker faces picked out grotesquely.

Jago stood in his corner. He had lost the toss and faced the light. The shadow of his opponent spanned the ring and was touching his feet. Vibart and D'Estin worked vigorously at his thighs and calves. Around the ring, but at a decent distance, the spectators waited, some seated, others in groups, all with mugs in hand. There was no tension here, no scramble to place bets. This was a local affair and if money changed hands it was between friends. The crowd was small for a fist-fight – perhaps eighty – and not much more than the usual attendance at the Fox on a Saturday.

Jago examined his hands. They were well prepared for their ordeal, hardened by vinegar and lemon, nails trimmed, knuckles greased. He was feeling fitter than he had all week, after forty-eight hours without aperients. And what he had lost in excess flesh he had replaced in muscle-fibre.

The difficulty lay in forcing himself to believe he was actually about to toe the scratch for a knuckle-fight, to flout the law he had been trained to uphold. After a week at Radstock Hall even Sergeant Cribb seemed a remote figure, as alien to this setting as his boxing coach at school. Certainly there was no sign of Cribb or Thackeray among the crowd. What would happen if the fight was raided by the local police, and they arrested him? Could Cribb intervene, or would the law take its course? Was the expulsion of one constable from the Force a matter worth sacrificing all their investigations for? Hadn't Thackeray himself suggested Cribb was callous towards his subordinates? He was a strange man, this Sergeant Cribb, and inspiring in his way; Jago wished he knew him well enough to trust him.

It was easier in this strange mood to believe that he was fighting for Mrs Vibart than Cribb. *Mrs?* It was Isabel from now on, she had told him when she came to the gym to see his final limbering that afternoon. 'You are fighting for me, Henry Jago,' she had said in that allusive way, inviting him to speculate on her meaning. 'I know that you will not disappoint me.' And she had put forward her hand and pressed his forearm. Little wonder that Cribb was fading as a source of inspiration.

'Will the two antagonists and attendants come to the scratch, please?'

To confirm the dreamlike nature of this experience, the referee was the landlord of the Fox. Jago was quite prepared for his opponent, whose face had been in shadow, to be Lydia's Papa, attended by the curate from St Martin's. Instead the man who stepped forward was a total stranger, Jago's height, but broader in the chest and bronzed from work in the fields. Instead of boxing-drawers he wore flannel long-johns artfully adapted, but obvious for what they were. If anyone felt uncomfortable it was Jago in the expensive white silk drawers Isabel had provided.

'Mr Jago?' said the landlord. 'We know each other, of course. This 'ere is Luke Judd from Benson's farm.' The rivals nodded in recognition. 'As to the rules, gentlemen, they are according to the London Prize-Ring, last amended 1866. Thirty seconds between rounds, and when I call "Time" you 'ave eight seconds to get to scratch unaided. No butting, gouging, biting, kicking or tearing the flesh with the fingernails. And no seizing of your antagonist below the waist or belting 'im when 'e's down. A man's down when 'e's got one knee and one 'and on the ground, and don't let me see no deliberate falling on each other. Seconds and bottle-'olders keep outside the ring until someone goes down. Then you can lift your man to 'is corner. The final matter to mention is that the referee gets five per cent of the takings, by the usual arrangements. No questions? Good. Retire to your corners and wait for the call of "Time".'

Everyone but the two fighters climbed out through the ropes. The imminence of action brought even the serious drinkers from the bar. Jago caught the surprised glance of one of the regulars. Last week he had been one of the window-seat group.

A light breeze fluttered the colours tied to the centre stake: black silk for Isabel. 'You are fighting for me, Henry Jago.' Was he the protégé – or she the prize?

'Time.'

Time of reckoning.

He walked to scratch and took his stance.

A fist jabbed at him. It was easy to jerk aside and respond with a probing left. Short of the target. He edged forward and measured the distance again. Judd rocked out of reach.

Judd was coming back, open to a straight left. A fast, no-nonsense punch direct to the point. Short, though! What was wrong? That should have floored him, not chucked him under the chin.

A sudden, vicious haymaker from Judd came perilously near. It fanned his ear as he leaned away. Then a second swing rammed his chest. He countered with one to Judd's ribs. Bone against bone. His knuckles smarted.

Pain transformed Judd into a threshing-machine. Arms flailed destructively, unstoppable. Most glanced off the forearms, but some Jago could not parry. He felt one jolt on his collar-bone. Another scraped his ear cruelly. 'They're almost as vulnerable as eyes to bare fists,' D'Estin had told him.

Now Judd was upon him, groping for a handhold. The grasp

for the throat was easy to deflect. But not the simultaneous crunch of the spiked boot on his foot.

Jago reeled in pain. A cuff on the temple. Balance gone. Down!

With astonishing speed D'Estin was through the ropes and hoisting him to the corner. Propped there on Vibart's knee, gasping for air.

'Drink this. Takes the pain away.'

Brandy and water, by the taste.

'Box the man. Don't let him wrestle you. Strike for the face.'

Agonized pulsation from the pierced foot.

'Time.'

Out to scratch again, to shoot a long right to Judd's head, warning him away. Beady brown eyes glinted in annoyance. 'Box the man.' Devilish hard with him waiting there, hands half open to grapple. Try though. A feinting right, and immediately a strong straight left. On the mark!

Judd winced and backed. Jago tried two more long lefts, more to intimidate than injure. Judd retreated again. A right. Judd was cornered, waiting for the onslaught.

Here was a chance for real advantage, not to be squandered. Coolly Jago set to work, measuring the punches and delivering them crisply. Judd bowed, arms locked across his face. Seeing no way past his attacker he clearly decided on a strategic closure of the round. Far from convincingly he tottered forward and fell at Jago's feet.

'Prettier work,' said D'Estin, as he sponged Jago's face. 'Don't finish him too early, though. You fight to instructions. Understand?'

Jago understood. Even in a backyard scuffle between two unknowns the ritual of the prize-ring had to be observed. You didn't finish a fight in three rounds.

So for the next five he fought to the book, controlling the bout as he pleased, treating the crowd to first blood in the sixth with a fine blow to Judd's swollen lip. In the seventh he allowed Judd to throw him down from a neck-hold. There was no difficulty now in believing in the reality of the fight; the spike wounds in his foot had greatly helped his concentration.

'You can give 'em a show of your quality in the next two, Jago, and finish it in the tenth, as we arranged,' D'Estin said between rounds. 'How are your knuckles?'

'Damned painful,' Jago told him, looking at them as detached objects resting on his thighs.

'Grip some oakum, then.' He pushed several strands of loose rope-fibre into the damp palms. 'It's quite within the rules, don't worry. It'll cushion your punching.'

As Jago rose from Vibart's knee he thought for a second that he recognized a face at an open window of the Fox. He had not been much aware of the crowd before; they supported Judd almost to a man, and he had ignored them. That face, though, was somehow familiar, and it watched him intently.

He gave his attention to Judd. The local man's strategy now was the desperate resort of attacking the neck. Early in his instruction from the Shoreditch professor Jago had learned how vulnerable the carotid artery was, either to persistent punching or to manual pressure. Fortunately the punches were slow in coming and he was able to deflect them easily. And as Judd in desperation bore down on him with fingers outstretched for a stranglehold, Jago turned his hip inwards, gripped his attacker's right arm and guided him across his hip into a cross-buttock. Judd crashed against one of the stakes and lay still.

'Neatly executed!' said D'Estin, genuinely pleased, when Jago returned to the corner. 'You're learning well.'

He was not listening. His attention had returned to the face at the window, for it had now been joined by another, easily recognizable as Sergeant Cribb. The first face *couldn't* be Thackeray's. It was entirely clean-shaven.

'Time.'

Out for the ninth. Judd was slow to scratch, barely within the eight seconds allowed. This would need to be a less punishing round, or he would never come out for the tenth. Not a blow had been exchanged when both men were distracted by shouts from outside the ring. The bombardment of mingled abuse and encouragement they had learned to accept. It was integral to the fight; they heard it and dismissed it.

This shouting carried a more urgent note that broke into the ritual. The fighters stood back from each other, and looked about them, trying to comprehend the scene. Spectators were abandoning the fight. Men were struggling to uproot the stakes. The ropes had already collapsed.

D'Estin was at Jago's side, wrapping a coat around him. 'The blues, man! Can't you hear? For God's sake get into the pub and hide. Here's your trousers.'

It was no time for a dignified exit. Jago could not see the police, but he sprinted for the door of the bar. He was *prima facie* evidence so was well looked after. Hands pushed him behind the bar counter and towards an open trapdoor. With difficulty (for he was still wearing spiked shoes) he descended a short ladder.

Below, it was pitch-black at first. His eyes had been straining against the sunset for the last half-hour. Judd's silhouetted form was imprinted on his retina, and now reappeared vividly in glowing orange in the darkness.

He felt a cask behind him and sat on it. The place was full of people, and more were trying to come down. Shivering, he pulled off the spikes and struggled into his trousers.

'Drink this. Do you good.' A tumbler was pushed into his hand. He gulped the contents thankfully.

Gradually, his eyes adapted themselves. He was in a spacious wine-cellar, rather larger than the ring he had just left, but there must have been forty men crammed in, talking in whispers. The trapdoor closed; it seemed inconceivable that the police should fail to search there.

'Quiet!' A stage-whisper from one of the last to descend.

Everyone waited. Jago could now distinguish Judd's bulk slumped across two barrels in obvious exhaustion. Most of the others were there. Judd's second and bottle-holder sat near him, taking turns to swig at his brandy bottle. D'Estin, the last to enter, stood on the ladder itself.

Footsteps crossed the floor above, deliberate, heavy steps that left no doubt as to the occupation of their maker. The voices were inaudible. The referee and a few gallant regulars were up there trying to bluff their way through. Everyone waited for the trap to be lifted, each working out an original reason for being there. Someone winked at Jago from across the cellar. Thackeray again? Or a travesty of Thackeray, for why ever should he shave off his whiskers?

Steps crossed again, several more this time, making the floor creak loudly. More voices.

Then silence.

Five agonized minutes.

The trap was lifted.

'All right, gentlemen. Out you come.' It was the landlord's voice.

They clambered up to daylight.

'Only Sam Dalton on 'is new tricycle,' the landlord was explaining. 'Coming over to show it off to me, 'e was. Brand-new 'Arrington Desideratum. Cost 'im fifteen quid. 'Ow 'e manages that on a bobby's income I don't know. Well, seeing that the fight was in progress as 'e rode up, poor old Sam 'ad no option but to stop it.'

'He gave us plenty of time to get down below,' said one appreciative voice.

'Yes, but 'e couldn't decently ignore the evidence,' said the landlord. 'We 'ad to leave five of the stakes in position. So Sam came in and questioned us. Most of us was regulars, so that was all right. 'E's taken two back to police 'ouse for questioning – Mr Vibart, because 'e tried to make a break for it on the dog-cart, you see; and that tall feller from London in the deer-stalker.'

Cribb arrested? Jago's eyes flew to one of the darkened chimney-seats, where the man who had winked was sitting. Jago now knew for certain that he was Thackeray. Although his face was in shadow, his eyes were visible. They glinted in quiet satisfaction.

Eight

Henry Jago sat in a state of bliss in a hip-bath at Radstock Hall. On Isabel Vibart's instructions the brine had been warmed to slightly below body-heat, and was ready in the changing-room when he returned. Two steaming jugfuls of water stood in reserve.

He winced at the colour of his knees jutting above water-level. Pugilism was dirty, as well as painful. He reached for a tablet of Pear's and began to lather the grazed and muddy skin. Beside the bath on a marble-topped table the entire resources of the bathroom were paraded – soaps, brushes, pumices, sponges and loofahs. On a lower tier stood a selection of oils, aromatic rubs and pomades in cut-glass containers. And, most welcome, a large glass of claret.

Jago took a sip of the drink and reclined, enjoying the luxury. Saws and severed heads could wait; tonight he had earned respite. To add piquancy to his enjoyment there was the thought of Sergeant Cribb in custody at Rainham police station. Cribb could not reveal his identity – particularly with Vibart there – so he would have to submit to interrogation by the local constable. Possibly even a night in the cells . . .

On further reflection the sergeant's predicament was worrying. Jago knew Inspector Jowett, 'Pilate', as he was unofficially known at the Yard. If it came to a point where a County Force complained to the Director, Jowett could be depended upon in only one respect. He would drop Cribb and his investigation like hot bricks. And if Cribb were in trouble for attending a prize-fight, what was the position of a constable who had *fought* one?

He felt surges of panic. Grotesque possibilities took shape in his brain. His hands gripped one side of the bath. 'The wretched man who stands before you in the dock, gentlemen of the jury, was once Scotland Yard's most brilliant young constable, a guardian of the law, entrusted with the confidential records of the Criminal Investigation Department. Expend no pity upon

him. There is no one so contemptible as a corrupt police officer.'
He pulled his hands away and put them to his forehead. When
he opened his eyes the fingers formed prison bars. He jerked
the hands down, splashing water in all directions.

It had really happened. He had appeared in a prize-ring. All
the time in his mind there had been the certainty of Cribb's
intervening at the last moment. He sponged his arms, trying to
calm himself. What regulations had he broken? He had not, in
effect, fought for money. 'It was strictly in the course of an investigation, your lordship. I was obeying orders.' 'Orders?
Whose orders?' 'Sergeant Cribb's.' 'Oh yes. I sentenced him
earlier this afternoon.'

He reached for the claret. Cribb! He had to believe that
Cribb would outwit the local police. Thinking otherwise was
inviting depression. How could he help the sergeant? Only by
controlling himself and quietly persevering with the inquiry.
How, though? Cribb wanted proof of the dismemberment. But
what was the use of searching for articles which would surely be
well-hidden, if not destroyed, by now? He had done his best, in
the little time available to him, to quarter the grounds on his
training runs, looking for likely burial spots for the severed
heads. Then D'Estin had told him to follow the same daily route.
He was not sorry; he rather preferred searching for the saw.

Would there be more opportunities for searching now that the
fight was over? He doubted it. They would have him in training for a second fight, encouraged by tonight's showing. He
would have to search the house by night, no matter how tired he
was. If he could find *some* kind of evidence – even papers, the
articles of battle, mentioning names – then he could send news
to Cribb and get out of this suffocating situation.

He was momentarily overwhelmed by a desire to be with
Lydia, sweet and untainted by all this. With a sense of shame
he realized she had been far from his thoughts for days. His
overtaxed mind struggled to create an image of her; all that came
was Isabel Vibart's gently mocking face.

He was jerked to awareness by D'Estin entering, bringing a
bathrobe.

'Don't sit there too long, Jago,' he said. 'Water softens the skin. How are your knuckles now?'

'A little numb.'

One of Jago's wrists was gripped and lifted, tong-like by the two digits on D'Estin's right hand.

'Bruised, merely. How about the rest of you? There was plenty of blood on you at the end. Mainly his, I hope.' D'Estin's tone was clinical. The close relationship between trainer and fighter had lasted no longer than the fight.

'I'm sorry I couldn't down him before the fight was stopped,' said Jago with conviction. Inwardly, he had baulked at the bludgeoning of a helpless opponent.

'It cost me fifty guineas,' D'Estin said. 'No fault of yours, though. We agreed on the tenth round. Had it been a first-class match we'd have had a clause in the articles to ensure the fight's continuance elsewhere. There's usually no question of a mill ending when the blues arrive. We simply move outside their boundary, set up the ropes again and resume. Isn't that right, Sylvanus?'

Jago had not noticed the Ebony's arrival. He was out of vision, somewhere behind the bath.

'Correct, Mr D'Estin.' A deep, educated voice.

'I'm sure that Henry knows all that, Robert.'

Good God! Isabel's voice!

Jago reached for a large sponge.

The embarrassment was all on his side. Isabel walked serenely across the room and seated herself on a bench.

'I am told you controlled the fight like a veteran, Henry,' she said. 'We are delighted with the promise that you showed to-night. When you are bathed and massaged I want you to dress for dinner. We always enjoy celebrating our successes, and you were close enough to victory to make no difference.'

'Fifty guineas. No difference,' muttered D'Estin.

She tossed her head in laughter.

'Really? Do you mean that I have *two* losers in my employment? Isn't it enough that Edmund should be so imbecile as to make a run for it when the police arrived? One middle-aged constable on a tricycle! What a fine testimony to the manly Vibarts!'

'He won't find it easy producing an explanation,' said D'Estin, as though Vibart deserved some sympathy. 'I know that bobby. He clings like a blasted leech until he's drawn the truth out of you.'

Her voice hardened. 'Edmund had better not say one word to the police, or I shall have him dealt with, brother-in-law or not. Now, Henry' – sweet reasonableness returned to the voice – 'you shouldn't stay too long in the water.'

Jago was determined to remain calm. He was, after all, a professional detective, and if nothing in his training had prepared him for this situation, that did not make it unsurmountable.

'I shall come out in a moment.'

A sceptical silence.

Jago soaped his knees for the second time. One simply had to prepare oneself mentally, to become detached. Of course one didn't climb out of a bath under a lady's scrutiny as a regular practice ...

The knees were spotless.

It would not do to spring out and make a bolt for the bathrobe. Something more dignified was called for.

He gripped the sides of the bath manfully and took a deep breath.

'For God's sake, Isabel,' said D'Estin. 'You can see the lad's not used to bathing in front of an audience.'

She laughed. 'He's trying to embarrass me, Henry.' She stood up arranging her dress. 'He hasn't succeeded, because I know you aren't ashamed of yourself. However, I must see to the preparation of the table. We shall meet in the rear dining-room tonight, gentlemen. Shall we say in one hour's time?'

Immediately she had gone Jago clambered out of the bath. D'Estin and the Ebony remained while he towelled himself energetically. He was used to communal changing-rooms, and their presence was not inhibiting. Not, that is, until he became conscious that the Ebony was studying his body. It was a steady, calculating gaze, as though each point of his physique were being assessed. For the first time since coming to Radstock Hall, Jago felt a strong impression that the Ebony was considering him as a rival.

Isabel's dinner-party was a revelation.

Meals were usually taken in a large dining-room at the front of the house, in sunlight for much of the day. The second dining-room, at the rear, was reserved for more special occasions.

D'Estin, more burly than ever in his dinner-jacket, greeted Jago with a glass of sherry.

'Amontillado, and an expensive one. Make the most of it, Jago. You'll be training again tomorrow. Sylvanus reckons to sink a dozen glasses on these occasions, don't you?'

The Ebony was standing in shadow, away from the candle-lit table. He made no response. Perhaps like Jago he resented the inference that pugilists came to sherry as horses to troughs of water.

Isabel had not appeared, and the other two were content to remain silent, so Jago stepped farther into the dining-room. He now saw in the play of candlelight that the small room was filled with objects from the East. Carvings, pottery, statuettes, bronzes: they seemed to have been deposited at the sides of the room with utter disregard for positioning or design. A large embroidered picture filled with semi-clothed Indian dancers surrounding a godlike figure was almost obscured by a grotesque figurine mounted on a plinth. On another wall two tigers' heads vied for space with a jewelled two-handed sword and a set of wood-carvings. Small tables and carved chests pushed to the walls were littered with silver, copper and ivory objects. Any one of them might have been a priceless artefact which a collector would have mounted in a showcase. Their very profusion in this small room led to an effect of depressing prodigality. The air was oppressive with the scent of sandalwood.

Hearing the rustle of silk, Jago turned.

'Do you like my Indian collection? It all belonged to my late husband.' She was dazzling, in a velvet dress of deep violet with a pale pink panel from bodice to hem. A row of tiny artificial flowers entwined her body, emphasizing, quite unnecessarily, the lines of her figure. 'He was there for some years, you know, exporting metalware. Some of these pieces are worth more than the house, he used to tell me. Do you like the necklace? He gave it to me as a birthday present.'

She approached Jago, for him to examine the golden pendant studded with rubies that rested in the cleft of her breasts. She subdued her voice to a murmur as she said, 'It is priceless.'

Jago looked at the jewel and was repelled. It was in the shape of a cobra poised to strike.

'You don't like serpents?' she said, sensitive at once to his reaction. 'What a good thing you weren't born an Indian, Henry Jago! In ancient India only the sacred cow was more revered among creatures. Perhaps you will allow me to wear it tonight, though.'

'It is a very fine piece,' said Jago, in some confusion.

They took their positions at table, a circular one draped in white linen fringed with minute beads. Among the silver table ornaments four black candles in glass funnels provided the only illumination. 'My colour, you know,' Isabel explained.

D'Estin was ordered to see to the champagne, which had been overlooked.

'We shall have the Roper Frères, 1874, Robert, if you please.' When he had left the room she added, 'He would bring an inferior vintage otherwise. Robert has a low opinion of everyone's palate but his own.' Each of her remarks was addressed to Jago; the Ebony might have been another statue for all the attention she gave him.

D'Estin returned, and a clear soup was served.

'Come here, Gruber,' Isabel commanded the maid, the same solemn woman who had first admitted Jago to the Hall. 'I want you to reassure Mr Jago. I think he secretly fears that the next course is curry.'

'Duck,' pronounced Gruber lugubriously. 'And chicken. And beef.'

After the main dish had been brought in under silver covers,

Gruber was dismissed. 'We serve ourselves on our celebration evenings,' Isabel explained. 'One feels less reserved with the servants out of the way.'

Jago wondered what she could possibly have in mind. He took a deep draught of champagne.

The joints were cooked in wine and smelt appetising. D'Estin and the Ebony took carvers and began to cut.

'You divide the duck, Henry,' Isabel said. 'Don't trouble with slices. Quarter it. We can forget Edmund.'

During the meal, the Ebony began to talk. In the previous week his speech had been limited to minimal responses. Now, made loquacious perhaps by the wine, he questioned D'Estin closely on the fight, demanding to know how each round had progressed. Jago did not intervene. His own memory was probably not reliable, anyway. He continued with his meal, enjoying at intervals an approving smile from Isabel as D'Estin described some highpoint of the action.

'Is he ready to fight me, then?' the Ebony demanded, when the account was finished.

'You?' Isabel exclaimed in astonishment. 'God, Sylvanus! You must be out of your mind!'

The Ebony threw down his knife and fork. 'And why? Why is it so extraordinary that he should fight me?'

'Stow your gammon, Morgan,' intervened D'Estin. 'How many fist-fights have you had in your time – twenty or thirty? This lad doesn't know a mill from a Morris dance yet. He wouldn't last two rounds in the ring with you. What are you bothered about? Haven't we paid you enough attention lately?'

Isabel glared at D'Estin.

'What am I bothered about?' repeated the Ebony. 'I'm a fighter. That's why I'm here. I want fights, not fancy parties!'

Isabel held herself in check. 'If that is really your attitude, Sylvanus, you need not stay.'

He was nodding his head. 'All right, then. I apologize.'

'A fight between you and Henry,' Isabel continued, 'would scarcely help any of us very much, even if you were evenly matched. Professionals fight for prize-money, not side-bets.

When we have an antagonist for you on the right terms you'll see some more action. Fighting every other week for silver won't further your career.' She was talking as his manager, putting her arguments with a force and purpose that should have detracted from her sexuality, but actually intensified it.

The Ebony had no answer.

'It's a pity you didn't join the other two at the police station, you ungrateful bastard,' commented D'Estin, insensitive to the electricity in the atmosphere. 'Then Jago and I might have enjoyed ourselves tonight, eh, Jago?'

Definitely time to vary the conversation.

'Who does the large statue represent?' he asked Isabel.

It had faced him all evening, glaring bolt-eyed from behind Isabel: a life-sized hag in bronze, bare-breasted and with four arms.

'This is Kali, the black earth-mother, Shiva's wife,' explained Isabel, in the manner of a drawing-room introduction. 'The Hindu goddess. Isn't she magnificent? She is said to dance among the slain on the battlefield and eat their flesh. This is her terrible aspect, but she can be very beautiful. I have a copper miniature of her over there somewhere, behind Sylvanus, in a most becoming form.'

Jago persevered. 'Why does she have four arms?'

'I really couldn't tell you. Some of the gods have more; Durga, another form of this same goddess, has ten. She uses them all, you see.'

Jago stood to examine the hideous figure more closely.

'These two are held forward,' he remarked. 'That would be to bless her followers, I expect?'

'Exactly! Do you see what the others are holding?'

The light was not good. Jago leant forward. 'This hand holds a weapon – a dagger, I think. And this one –' His voice trailed away.

'It is rather gruesome, isn't it?' said Isabel blithely. 'She is holding the severed head of a giant, dripping blood. Percy once told me the story, but I cannot be sure of all the details now. She developed a thirst for blood quite involuntarily, poor thing.

She killed a demon – a perfectly proper thing for a goddess to do – but Brahma had granted a special boon that every drop of the demon's blood that was shed would create thousands more like him. What could Kali do but drink every drop herself?'

'I suppose so.'

'If you look closely, you'll see her ornaments. She has earrings made of little children, and three necklaces: one of skulls, another of the heads of her sons, and another' – she paused significantly – 'of a snake.'

There was silence in the room. Jago turned to look at Isabel. She was smiling, the tiny ruby-eyes at her throat glinting in the candlelight.

'My candid opinion, if you want it, is that it's a deuced ugly piece of furniture,' said D'Estin, breaking the tension. 'I don't know why you keep it, unless it's to scare the likes of Jago and Sylvanus here. Even the fist-fighters *I* train aren't equipped to square up to a four-armed fighting woman. Don't it give you nightmares, Sylvanus?'

The Ebony was grim-faced. 'She is the death-goddess. It is foolhardy to provoke her.'

D'Estin's fist thumped on the table. 'God! He really believes in it! Black magic, eh, Sylvanus? Mumbo Jumbo!' He rocked back in his chair laughing, but it was the laugh of a man trying to convince himself of his own immunity to the atmosphere.

'No, Robert,' said Isabel coldly. 'Not Mumbo Jumbo. Dark, evil deeds are committed in Kali's name. Unspeakable obscenities and sacrificial killings. She is a very potent goddess of death.'

D'Estin grunted contemptuously and felt into his waistcoat pocket. 'As I would appear to have offended the gods, I'll have a last cigar, then – if you and Madam Kali will permit, that is.'

Jago returned to his chair. New topics of conversation! The atmosphere was more highly charged than when he had intervened to relieve it.

The cigar fumes now blended with the heady aromas of sandalwood and wine. Smoke writhed and swirled amorphously before spreading into horizontal planes above their heads. Jago's eyelids smarted. The fumes were tricking his vision. The scarcely discernible figure of the goddess appeared to reach through the haze, beckoning.

'What was that?'

The mesmeric atmosphere had been disturbed by the slamming of a door in another part of the house. Isabel's question was swiftly answered. The door behind Jago was thrust open by Edmund Vibart.

'So! I might have realized nobody would think of coming out to Rainham for me.'

He was flushed with annoyance.

'To join you at the police station?' D'Estin said sarcastically. 'I didn't think the rest of us were invited. What did they serve – meat or poultry?'

Vibart openly struggled to control his fury. 'The bloody trap. You drove off with the bloody trap. How was I going to get back?'

'You could have borrowed the constable's tricycle.'

He stepped in anger towards D'Estin, his fists clenched. The trainer rose and leered down at him, cigar in hand, inviting aggression.

'That will do, Robert.' Isabel spoke with quiet authority. 'Fetch another chair, will you Sylvanus? Now, Edmund, sit down and tell us what happened.'

'What do you think happened? I told him I was drinking in the bar and knew nothing about the fight.'

'He questioned you?'

'Extensively. I told him nothing except my name and address, which he knew anyway. Finally, he agreed to let me go. I think he wanted to spend more time questioning the other cove.'

'Who was that?' Isabel asked.

'The tall 'un from London.'

'Not one of the Beckett mob?' asked D'Estin.

'God, no. This was one of the gentry. A nobby-looking cove in a deerstalker and Norfolk.'

Jago mentally noted the description. Cribb would savour it.

'What was he doing at the Fox tonight?' Isabel asked.

Vibart shrugged. 'Why ask me? See Constable Dalton in the morning. That old leech'll be catechizing him all bloody night. There won't be much he can't tell you by tomorrow. Have you drunk all the champagne?'

Jago's depression returned. How could Cribb give a convincing explanation when he was so obviously a stranger in the area? Constable Dalton didn't sound like a man easily taken in. What if Cribb were charged?

His attention was brought back to the conversation. Vibart was asking Isabel for money.

'Look, it's only thirty I want. I lost a level pony on that deuced fight, and it cost me a sov to get brought back here. You said you'd pay each time I was bloody bottle-holder.'

'You shall get your fee at the proper time,' she said with contempt. 'What you lose on wagers is not my concern.'

Enmity flashed between them. Vibart snatched up a silver statuette. 'I'll take this, then, if you haven't the ready money. All these bloody trinkets should be mine by rights, anyway.'

Speaking deliberately, Isabel said: 'You will replace that figurine on the mantelshelf or I shall tell Robert to break your arm.'

There was no doubt in anyone's mind about Isabel's determination. Nor did anyone doubt D'Estin's willingness to cooperate.

Vibart flung down the ornament and left the room.

In the silence after, Jago detected a quickening in Isabel's breath. Her lips parted fractionally. Her shoulders jerked. She was giggling like a schoolgirl. Finally she tossed her head and laughed convulsively.

D'Estin, too, was smiling.

'It was most uncivil of you to take the trap,' she scolded him, still vibrating with amusement. 'After he'd given Henry his knee for nine rounds too. He was exhausted! How you could sit here, Robert, enjoying your roast duck and thinking of Edmund possibly legging it back across the fields, I cannot understand!' Laughter rippled from her again.

'If he hadn't tried to abandon us in the first place, he wouldn't have been caught,' said D'Estin. 'That's so, ain't it, Jago. Look alive, man!'

Jago tried to appear animated.

'Of course, you must be used up!' Isabel said. 'While we prattle on with our ridiculous family jokes the hero of the evening wilts away! Your poor flesh, Henry! Are you terribly stiff from your exertions?'

Here was the cue for an exit. 'Somewhat,' Jago agreed.

'Then you will want massaging. It will relax you before sleep. Take him to the morning-room, Robert. The chaise-longue will do.'

'No thank you, D'Estin,' Jago hastily intervened. 'I think I'll just retire. You won't want to massage me as late as this.'

'Me?' said D'Estin. 'You think I'm the masseur? With this?' He held out his mutilated hand. 'No, my friend. Isabel will tone you up. Don't think she isn't strong enough, eh, Sylvanus?'

The Ebony said nothing, whether from fatigue or for his own reasons.

'It really isn't necessary,' Jago protested.

'I shall enjoy it,' Isabel said.

'There's no escape, you see,' D'Estin pointed out.

'I think I should like to sleep, if you don't mind.'

'You will sleep more comfortably if your muscles are loosened.'

Jago struggled for a stronger excuse.

D'Estin came to the rescue. 'The lad's totally spent, Isabel. I think we should let him get to bed, as he says.'

She smiled at the wilting pugilist. 'Very well. Good night to you, Henry, and thank you for acquitting yourself so capably today.'

Jago at once stood to go. The Ebony, too, nodded and removed himself, leaving Isabel and D'Estin alone. It was well past midnight. The candles had burned to a molten liquid at the bottom of each glass. D'Estin's cigar glowed against the weird background like a demon's eye.

'You didn't get your way, did you?' he said.

'What do you mean by that?'

'You know what I mean. You wanted to get your hands on his body. You can't resist the feel of a man's flesh, can you? Tired, bruised flesh that you can knead back to vitality.'

She was angry. 'Don't speak in that way.'

'Is that why you watch them through your peep-hole as they work in the gym? Do you like to see them suffer, Isabel?'

'You're mad!' she cried in agitation. 'I want the best performance out of the fighters we keep here. They have to be watched, or they won't work. It's for their own good. I want no more failures among my pugilists. The last episode was all too sordid.'

D'Estin breathed cigar-smoke across the table. 'It doesn't sound very convincing, Isabel. We both know the truth. Why try to conceal it? That isn't a training regimen you devise for them each morning. It's a sentence of punishment meticulously planned so that they suffer progressively more from day to day. It has nothing to do with fist-fighting. Power – that's the point of it, isn't it? No need for you to bother yourself with women's rights and such nonsense. You get all the self-esteem you want watching strong men shake with fatigue at your whim.'

'I won't have you talk in this way –'

'There's no need to agitate yourself,' said D'Estin coolly. 'I'm not the only one in this house to see why you do it. You've noticed the way the black looks at you, haven't you? He knows as well as either of us. That's why you turn to new prey. But Jago has eluded you for tonight at least, so . . .' He stubbed out the cigar with deliberation . . . 'you can take notice of me. I've waited too long.'

'For heaven's sake, Robert!' she said, uncertain how to treat him.

He stood and pulled her from the chair and into an embrace. His mouth clamped on hers. She jerked herself free.

'Don't tell me you're too weary,' D'Estin snarled. 'You never used to be. You'd have been willing if Jago had found the strength.'

Her hand swung through the semi-darkness and slapped his

face, catching him more on the temple than the cheek. It gave the final impetus to his aggression. He caught her arm with his maimed hand, and with the other successively wrenched the dress and undergarments from her shoulders. Then he forced her to the carpet. Above them the dying candlelight played on the grinning features of Kali.

When it was over, D'Estin held her for some seconds. There was tenderness in his whisper. 'It need not have been so, my love. We should never have allowed misunderstandings to destroy what was so precious.'

But she was looking past him, at the statue, and her voice was expressionless. 'You chose an appropriate setting, Robert. Our relationship is dead – dead for ever.' She pushed him from her as though he were some unwanted counterpane and began fastening her clothes. 'Forget that I ever showed you affection.' As she got to her feet clasping the torn dress to her, he crouched, watching, cowed by her self-possession. 'And remember that only a fool forces himself on women when he can give them no pleasure whatsoever.'

Nine

Constable Thackeray reported early at the Waterloo Road Police Station on Monday morning. Whatever happened that day he was resolved not to offend Cribb. The constable's impish pleasure in his sergeant's predicament after the fight had drained away rapidly. Prometheus unchained was no more alarming than Cribb humiliated.

Mercifully, Sunday had provided time for the fury to subside. So far as police duties were concerned, Cribb was a strict sabbatarian. He arrived as jaunty as ever, tossing his bowler and umbrella deftly on to the stand.

'Well, Thackeray. What has Monday brought?'

The breezy manner was encouraging.

'One letter from Rainham, Sarge – Jago's handwriting. And a

young lady to see you. Miss Boltover, daughter of Colonel Boltover.'

'Don't know her,' said Cribb, raising his eyebrows. 'What does she want?'

'She won't say, Sarge. She is rather agitated. She's a handsome-looking lass, too.'

'Red-headed?'

'Why, yes,' confirmed Thackeray in surprise.

'Ask the constable on duty to make some cocoa. Women with hair that colour have temperaments to match, Thackeray. She'll need calming down before we ask her in here.'

Calming down with cocoa? Was this the intrepid Cribb? Possibly his recent experience had taken its toll. Thackeray went on his errand.

When he returned, Cribb was deep in Jago's letter, which seemed a long one.

'Self-pity,' he said at last, putting it down. 'Very regrettable in a police officer. I thought young Jago was stouter-hearted. This could present problems.' He tapped his nose with a pen-holder. 'You saw him after the fight. What sort of shape was he in?'

'He looked tired, Sarge, and no wonder. He didn't appear to be injured much, except for a slight limp. The second – the big one with the fingers missing –'

'D'Estin.'

'– got him into a trap and drove him away as soon as we came up from the cellar. He looked somewhat startled when the landlord told us you and Vibart were arrested.'

'Startled me, too,' admitted Cribb, ready apparently to relate the painful incident. 'Took me till almost midnight to get myself released.'

'How did you possibly manage it?' asked Thackeray, primed to flatter. 'It was an appalling situation, Sarge.'

'Most certainly was. I couldn't say anything while Vibart was there. Had to wait while he talked himself out of it. A deuced long time he took, too.'

'What did you say when you were alone with the village bobby, Sarge? Did you admit you were in the Force?'

'Good Lord, no! He'd have checked with the Yard. If Jowett heard I'd been arrested that would be the end of our investigations. Possibly a public inquiry. We're in a very delicate position, Constable. Don't you forget it.'

'How did you get away, then?' asked Thackeray, honestly rather baffled.

'I took the measure of the man as he questioned Vibart. Fine officer, in his way. Pertinent questions. Two things were clear, though. First, he hadn't meant to break up the prize-fight; he didn't know it was on. Second, he didn't want to lose the respect the locals held him in. So I planned my strategy, and waited for him to release Vibart.'

'Vibart thought of an alibi, did he, Sarge?'

'Nothing so grand as that. He got sent home eventually though.'

'I expect he would, being a local man,' remarked Thackeray, following Cribb's theme most attentively.

'Exactly. I was different, though. A stranger, you see. No one in Rainham was going to shed tears over me if I landed in the courts. So I couldn't simply rely on an alibi. I had to go on the offensive.'

'Attack his weak points?'

'Yes. I said I was from the *Illustrated Sporting* – down from London to report the fight. I asked him what his name was – took the questioning over before he'd begun, you see?'

Thackeray could well believe it.

'I told him he'd figure in the headlines in my newspaper. "Prize-fight at Rainham Stopped by Police". That delighted him. I could see him picturing his Inspector at the County Office reading it. Then I told him what the report would say – that one spectator was arrested, and about a hundred, including the main participants, walked away.'

'That must have made him reconsider,' said Thackeray, feeling for the man.

'Not sufficiently, though,' continued Cribb. 'He was a stubborn cove. I told him my newspaper could stop all prize-fighting in the district. We had only to announce that the blues were keen to make arrests there. That finally defeated him. The fury of his drinking friends was a bigger threat than an angry inspector. He made me promise not to print a word and let me go.'

'Incomparable!' said Thackeray, and meant it.

Cribb turned to other matters.

'Miss Boltover. Let's see what she wants. I hope she's calmer after her Cadbury's.'

Thackeray ushered her in. She was pale and her eyes darted nervously about the room, but she composed herself sufficiently to arrange her dress as she sat in the chair Cribb provided. Thackeray took her parasol.

'My father contacted Scotland Yard,' she began when the introductions were made, 'and Inspector Jowett said that you could be found here.'

Thackeray gulped.

'You wished to find me, in particular?' inquired Cribb.

She was on the verge of tears. 'Henry Jago – Constable Henry Jago – is a close acquaintance of ours. Can you tell me where he is?'

'I fear not at present,' said Cribb at once. 'Are you concerned on his behalf? I think he is quite well.'

She took a folded newspaper from the bag on her lap. 'Read that please – the part I have marked.'

Cribb glanced at the headline 'INCONCLUSIVE MILL IN THE SOUTH ESSEX DISTRICT BETWEEN LUKE JUDD AND HENRY JAGO, A NOVICE'. He read it twice more before pushing the newspaper to Thackeray. It was nightmarish.

'How did you find this?' he asked, his mind racing through the implications.

'It is my father's newspaper –'

'He knows? The Colonel!'

'I don't think so. He only reads the cricket scores. I saw the newspaper lying on a table, and Henry's name seemed to leap at me from the page. It *is* my Henry, isn't it?'

Cribb confirmed that it was. 'He hasn't deserted, Miss. We know all about this. He's doing important work.'

Lydia's eyes dilated. 'You know! But it's barbarous, this fighting with bare fists! It's illegal!'

'I'll thank you to modulate your voice, Miss. Not many in this office are privy to this investigation. We wouldn't want to place Jago – Henry, that is – in a difficult spot.'

'It is in the newspaper. I should think everyone has seen it by now.'

Cribb coughed awkwardly. 'No disrespect to your father, Miss – not everyone reads *Bell's Life*. Besides, there's few that will associate this with *our* Jago.'

She snatched the paper from Thackeray. 'There's no doubt who it is if you read this. "Jago, alias D'Estin's Novice, is certainly the largest twelve-stone man we ever saw, especially his arms, which are literally full of muscle; his attitude is very good, and particularly easy; perhaps, however, too slender loins, and is very slim on his understandings." That is Henry, Sergeant!'

'I don't deny it, Miss,' said Cribb. 'You recognize him from the description and so do we. So does his doctor, I expect, if he reads *Bell's*. But there ain't many others who can tell a man from the shape of his arms and legs.'

She coloured.

'You'll have watched him swimming in the Serpentine, I dare say,' said Cribb, with prompt tact. 'The truth of the matter is, Miss, that he's sending us reports on certain suspicious persons. He does the knuckle-fighting to give himself a reason for being there, so to speak. Pugilism's as harmless as tin soldiers to a man of his experience.'

'Harmless!' Lydia went back to the newspaper, and began to read aloud: ' "Round one – The attitude of the men being struck, they sparred long for an opening until Judd dashed in his left on the body. Jago retaliated with a flush hit to the ribs, which caused Judd to commence business in earnest, and within seconds the novice's neck and shoulders were as red as pickled cabbage. A spanking hit with the dexter mawley on Jago's left listener had him staggering. Then a stinger with the left on the knowledge-box completely knocked him off his pins to mother earth." Harmless!'

'Capital writing, though!' cried Cribb. 'What do they say about the other rounds?'

Lydia tossed the paper aside. 'It was too revolting to read. I simply cast my eyes to the foot of the column to ensure that Henry was not killed.'

Thackeray had now got the paper. 'This is a more refreshing bit, Miss. "Round six – Jago at once planted a right with terrific force on the masticator. It was a staggerer and so bothered Judd that he was unable to escape a clinker on the ivories, bringing 'first blood,' the crimson tide soon flowing copiously. A nasty one on the bridge of Judd's smelling-bottle caused the cork to be drawn there. Good counter-hitting to a close, when Judd got to grass." ' He beamed at Lydia.

She grimaced.

'He's well able to protect himself, Miss Boltover,' Cribb assured her. 'Nor was he hurt in the least. When he comes back there won't be a mark on him, and with any luck he'll have tracked down a' – he checked himself – 'suspected person.'

'But how long does he have to persist with this dreadful pose as a prize-fighter?'

'Not long now.' Cribb suddenly had an inspiration. 'You want to get in touch with him, I expect?'

'Please, oh yes!'

The sergeant leaned forward confidentially. 'If I let you write to him he might be able to reply. I couldn't give you his address, of course. But you could write a letter, and we would see to its delivery.'

Her face fell a little. 'Just a letter?'

'Nothing else would be safe at this stage, Miss. And I shall have to read the letter, you understand.'

'Oh.'

'And you won't mind me including a few lines of my own? You could write 'em for me, you see. It's a way of getting a message to him.'

Minutes later, Lydia sat with pen and paper in another room. At the desk opposite was a young constable with walrus moustache and eyes more sinister than any on the 'Wanted' notices behind him. 'As tender a letter as you can write,' Cribb had ordered. 'And don't mind us, Miss.'

Thackeray read Jago's report.

'He sounds uncommon depressed, Sarge. Seems to think he's done all he can at Rainham. It's my belief that he's missing the company of a certain young woman.'

Ascribing motives was a favourite occupation with Thackeray. Cribb might have been more impressed if he had not earlier noticed his assistant's eyes straying to a partially uncovered ankle.

'Miss Boltover doesn't really come into it,' he declared with a tinge of reproof. 'Jago's too smart a bobby to let sentiment spoil his work. What worries him is what the Ebony told him on Saturday night after the meal in the Indian room. If the black really plans to quit Radstock Hall Jago becomes the principal fighter. Everything is centred on him, you see – training, matches. Possibly the widow's attention in other respects.'

'Do you believe that, Sarge? Why should the Ebony want to leave? He's well looked after where he is. The training couldn't be more lavish.'

'Financial considerations,' said Cribb. He picked up the letter and read: ' "Morgan (The Ebony) told me he was not going to stay much longer at Radstock Hall and if I was wise I would not remain either. He said that evil things were liable to happen here. He had made his plans to leave, and Edmund Vibart was helping him. Mrs Vibart wasn't the only backer of knuckle-fighters, and others were willing to pay handsomely for a star performer." From which I deduce that Vibart has acted as agent for the Ebony with another group of backers.'

'The roughs that managed Meanix?'

'Quite possibly. There aren't that many parties interested in managing knuckle-fighters.'

'Why should Vibart cheat his sister-in-law?' asked Thackeray.

'You *did* read the letter?' snapped Cribb. 'The man is short of money. Someone will pay him well for seducing the black away from Mrs Vibart. He promised the Ebony larger rewards and more regular fights. It doesn't require any more persuading than that to get him away from Radstock Hall.'

Put that way, it made sense to Thackeray.

'As for Jago's low spirits,' continued Cribb, 'Miss Boltover's letter will raise them if it's spiced with a few sharp instructions from me. He stays at Rainham for at least another week. I need evidence, and a shake-up at Radstock Hall may provide it.'

Ten

Henry Jago put down his book and listened. Listened for anything but the susurration of beech leaves in the grounds outside. An hour and a half had passed since Vibart's evening recital had finished and the bolts were secured downstairs, and Gruber, the German maid-servant, had shuffled to her quarters at the rear of the house. There had been sounds enough after that – creaks and murmurs, howls and whines – but none of recognizable human origin.

He looked at his watch. No need to light the candle tonight; the sky outside was clear, the moon in its third quarter. Mendoza's *Memoirs,* prescribed reading for any literate fist-fighter, lay open on the counterpane, the words legible even in partial shadow. Tonight, though, the Jew's exploits ninety years before were insufficiently diverting. It was earlier than Jago had planned, but he decided to start. He got up, drew a bathrobe over his nightshirt, and crept across the room. On the mantel-shelf, in front of Blondin, was an Indian club. He pushed the narrow end up his right sleeve as far as the elbow so that the bulbous part rested in his palm. Then he eased open the door of his room.

The landing led past the Ebony's door for some twenty-five yards to the entrance of Isabel's suite, guarded by a suit of tarnished armour at the head of the main staircase. The room between was now unoccupied, D'Estin having moved on Sunday to a bedroom beyond Jago's, up a small flight of stairs and around a corner in the passage. The floor was carpeted, but beneath the comforting pile lay boards as ready to screech as nesting game-fowl. Jago moved with a poacher's stealth. He had tried every board before, and knew which of them were stable.

Once past Isabel's door, the stairs were easier. They were noisy only on the banister side. He descended quickly and crossed the hall to the passageway leading to the kitchen. This would be difficult; he had been there only once before on the pretext of asking for a lemon for his skin. He hoped that the cook, another foreign woman seldom seen outside, kept the place in good order. Any kitchen implement accidentally knocked to the stone floor would sound an alarum through the house.

Jago tapped the door inwards. It groaned. There was no avoiding that. He paused momentarily, and went in. Fortunately the moonlight had penetrated there. A wedge of bluish white divided the room diagonally from window to skirting-board, chancing on a row of copper saucepans and highlighting them. He crossed the floor like an intruder in an illuminated tableau. He had seen what he came for: a large board over the stove with twenty or thirty hooks, from which labelled keys were suspended. He was unlikely to be heard, but he took excessive care not to chink them as he selected the one he needed. He pocketed it and turned his attention to the meat safe. From the lower shelf he removed a sizeable piece of steak. Its absence would not be noticed, for the safe was prodigally over-stocked. He withdrew the Indian club from his sleeve to free both hands and then wrapped the meat in cheese-cloth and put it into his bathrobe pocket. Then he slipped the bolt on the kitchen door, picked up the club and stepped outside the house.

A walk of thirty or more yards separated the house from the woodshed, where Jago was going. No distance at all, unless one recalled D'Estin's earthy warning: 'If you want the privy at night, forget it. Dogs, y'know. Better to wait till morning.' It had not been easy heeding the advice in those first painful nights after the physicking, but occasional baying from the grounds had proved a strong disincentive. It said much for his present determination to find the evidence Cribb wanted that he was now taking his chance with the dogs. Whether this indicated loyalty to Cribb or desperation to end his stay at the Hall Jago did not like to contemplate. He gripped the Indian club and stepped manfully across the open yard to the shed.

Damn! The key was difficult to fit in. Or was he too nervous? It turned after a fearful delay and with a huge gasp of relief he stepped into the shed and slammed the door closed. Never mind silence now!

Half the building was stacked with logs cut into foot-lengths. He couldn't possibly spend the night unstacking them to look for severed heads, although one could well be hidden there, perhaps under the ground, which was simply earth. He sniffed; there was only the expected smell of sawn timber. Nor was there much hope of finding bloodstains among these layers of soil and sawdust. There was one more possibility: the saw. If he could somehow smuggle that to Cribb an expert might detect human blood particles somewhere on its surface. But where was it – hanging up somewhere?

Jago turned. There *was* a saw suspended from a nail on the wall behind him. In fact there were twelve saws, of all sizes and varieties. He swore aloud.

As if in answer there came a low, prolonged snarl from outside. The sweat on his body was suddenly chilled and a pulse was thrumming in his temple. He kept absolutely still.

The beast – if it was only one – was circling the shed. He heard its rhythmic panting progress purposefully along the outer walls. It knew he was there. He could stay its prisoner till morning; or he could take his chance on getting back.

There was a small ventilation window high on one wall adjacent to the door. Jago slowly forced it open. The hound was under it in an instant, growling menacingly, ready to leap if his hand should venture outside.

He had to take the chance. From his pocket he took the steak and unwrapped it. He went close to the window. The aperture was depressingly small. With all the momentum he could gather at so fine an angle he slung the meat into the scrub behind, perhaps ten yards from the shed. Without waiting to check whether the dog had moved he flung open the shed door and bolted across the yard, appallingly vulnerable in his flowing nightshirt and robe.

But he was at the kitchen door and inside and the bolt was across before he heard anything from the dog. Outside, the entrance to the shed gaped, the key still in the swinging door. He went to bed. Explanations could wait.

The summons to report to Isabel next morning was no surprise to Jago. But its purpose was.

She was in the morning-room at her writing-desk, and she did not look up when he entered. It was early; one rarely saw her before noon. She was wearing black, as usual, velveteen skirt and sealskin jacket over a white lace blouse. Her wardrobe must have been bought for a year's mourning, at least. Only on the evening after his fight had Jago seen her in another colour.

He coughed discreetly.

She continued with her writing for perhaps a minute. When she eventually spoke she did not look at Jago.

'You have disappointed me, Henry.'

He felt sure he knew why. 'Disappointed?'

'Yes. I thought you understood that we have to keep our activities here entirely confidential.'

'I *do* understand that.'

She turned to face him. Inconsequentially he reflected that she probably wore black for its dramatic effect. Her face was radiant, the line of her cheek and neck in sharp relief against the sleek cut of the jacket collar.

'This letter arrived for you.'

'Letter?' It was not possible. Only Cribb knew where he was.

'Don't try to appear surprised, Henry. You must have invited her to write to you. Oh, I know all about your Lydia. It was necessary for me to read the letter, you understand. I cannot countenance my fighters corresponding clandestinely. Didn't we have an understanding that you told nobody where you were?'

This was incomprehensible. 'Yes.'

'And now you break your word. How many letters have you written to her?'

What on earth should he say?

'One.'

'Then you will write one more, and only one. You will tell Miss Boltover that it will be safer for you both if she does not attempt to correspond with you. From time to time she can read about your progress in the sporting newspapers, as she appears to have done on this occasion. But she must learn not to indulge her sentiments in other respects. If she really intends to marry you, as you suppose, she will wait. When you have earned some good purses with me she will be glad enough that she was patient. She at least has prospects. Other women have none. Here is your letter.'

He stepped forward and took it. The handwriting was Lydia's, he was sure. What in Heaven's name was Cribb doing?

'I apologize. I did not like deceiving you.'

Isabel had picked up her pen again. 'I should like to see your reply when you have written it.'

'You shall,' Jago assured her, turning to withdraw.

'And Henry.' She spoke without looking up. 'So that you shall have an opportunity of demonstrating your loyalty I have instructed Robert to extend your training exercises today. Now you may go.'

Sergeant Cribb had the devil of a lot to answer for.

An hour later Jago, sweat coursing down the sides of his nose and on to his naked chest, was suspended from the wall-bars, periodically raising his knees to D'Estin's command. The white drawers made the work increasingly difficult as his body temperature rose; the damp silk clung to his body and seemed tauter over knees and loins with every movement.

'Get them higher, man!'

Thank God there had been no mention of the wood-shed! Perhaps the servants had not reported the unlocked door, thinking they were concealing each other's carelessness.

'Right! Down you come! Take the bar-bells and begin squatting and rising. Nimble's the word!'

This would be easier. The abdominal muscles would get relief even if the thighs ached. In certain respects he was content to take his punishment, for punishment this most certainly was, whatever Isabel termed it. Earlier, his resentment had been strong. Now, after briefly reading Lydia's letter he was less angry; even a little encouraged. Paramount, of course, was the pleasure in recognizing that most of the letter was genuinely hers; at times this last week she had seemed very remote. Now her concern and affection heartened him.

'Get into a rhythm, Jago! Don't rest on your haunches!'

Cribb's message, cunningly phrased (he supposed, as it was palpably not Lydia's style) and inserted in Lydia's handwriting, was also encouraging. 'It seems insufferable that you must be away so long, but I know how important it is to your career and our prospects. Please, Henry, endure whatever is necessary for both our sakes, but be wary too (in the ring). Learn all that you can at Radstock Hall, for it will help later. But you must not concern yourself unduly about me. Remember that I am not so far away, and when you fight, rest assured that I shall know about it and shall not let you out of my thoughts.' Surely the tenderest message Cribb had ever sent to a constable.

'Very well! Now the dumb-bells, if you please. Above the head. Lower them slowly. Elbows straight!'

The pain in his biceps was just endurable. He could not continue long. The weights started to pull the arms down from the crucifix pose.

'Keep them up, man! You're on show, you know!'

On show ... Something in D'Estin's emphasis confirmed what Jago had increasingly suspected: that concealed somewhere in the panelled wall ahead of him was an observation-hole. Each exercise was staged facing that end of the gymnasium. Every grimace, every agonizing effort, was scrutinized by its architect, Isabel Vibart.

'That will do,' D'Estin ordered. 'You can finish with the Wrestler's Bridge.'

The devil he would. Once before they had bullied him into that. The pain was excruciating. And that was when he was fresh. It sounded simple enough, like touching one's toes. One lay on the ground with legs bent and forced one's back and buttocks up so that all the weight rested on heels and head. 'Like a wrestler avoiding being thrown,' they had told him. 'You keep it up for ten seconds.' He had collapsed in six.

'The Wrestler's what?' Any time now was precious.

'You know very well! Get down! Orders!'

'On the contrary, I don't know.'

'I'm sure you've done it. You've seen Morgan do it, anyway. There's only one way to learn properly.' D'Estin picked up a boxing-shoe and placed it, spikes upward, on the ground. 'You make a back over that for ten seconds. Then I kick it away. There isn't a mark on Morgan's back anywhere. Where is the black bastard? He was told to report sharp at noon.'

What was the point of silence?

'He will not be reporting.'

D'Estin frowned. 'What do you mean by that?'

'You won't see Sylvanus today. He walked out with his baggage after breakfast. It was obvious to anyone that he was not coming back.'

'Walked out?' One would think from D'Estin's tone that Radstock Hall was a pleasure-garden. Recovering from sheer disbelief, he hurried across to the dressing-room door. 'God! You must be right! I must see Isabel.'

Jago hobbled away to get into a cold bath.

Later, he lay in bed, sore and stiff, but not entirely displeased with the day. The afternoon, once he realized D'Estin was too preoccupied to supervise the 'training', was positively diverting. When the Ebony's room had been checked pandemonium broke loose in the house. Panicking servants – and in German the panic was formidable – roamed the house checking the valuables. D'Estin was sent in the dog-cart in pursuit of the deserter, but returned later, with the news that a 'strong-looking man of colour' had been seen boarding the London train soon after eleven. Then came the inquisition: D'Estin, Vibart and finally Jago appearing before Isabel. She was tight-lipped when he saw her, but surprisingly forbearing with him. Perhaps Vibart had managed to convince her that the Ebony had left of his own accord. At any rate, Jago was able to withdraw after ten minutes, having admitted to no more than seeing the departure – which had actually been quite conspicuous, but exceedingly well-timed. And by supper that evening calm was restored, if a little uneasily. Isabel said little to D'Estin or her brother-in-law, but talked freely to Jago about the war in Afghanistan, the theatre, the London season – anything, in fact, but pugilism. At nine he had been able to plead tiredness. For one alarming moment he thought she was about to offer massage, but it passed. He thankfully made his exit.

And now it was night again, and he lay listening. He had woken from two hours' sleep, necessary and convenient, for it spared him the nervous strain of waiting. By now the house was reassuringly quiet; only the pleasant rustle of rain outside breaking absolute silence. Enough to smother a creaking floorboard.

Painful as it was, he had to rouse himself. A curious sentence in Lydia's letter, after he read it for the fourth time, thinking more of Cribb than Lydia (exceedingly difficult), had stayed in his mind. His tired brain had made enough sense of it before he fell asleep to ensure that he would not sleep long. 'Your suggestion that I might divert myself by corresponding with my cousin Roberta in the Midlands has had an encouraging result, for last week I received a reply from Birmingham full of support and news – just what I needed at the present time.' Once it dawned on him that Roberta was the Chief Constable of Birmingham – Cribb would be priding himself on that inspiration – he deciphered the rest. The headless pugilist had been identified. All he now had to do at Radstock Hall was discover some clear evidence linking the murdered man with D'Estin, Vibart or Isabel, or perhaps all three. He felt certain it was there – documentary evidence, articles of battle, or even a diary of training – somewhere downstairs, and probably in Isabel's writing-desk.

So he opened the door of his room and crept cautiously along the landing. Past the now empty room where the Ebony had slept. On as far as the door of the room adjoining Isabel's. There he paused, deciding the points on the carpet where each foot could safely press. Then forward again, gliding lightly for a large man. The merest glance, as he passed, at Isabel's door. Did her obsession with black extend to her night-attire – the sheets of her bed, even? Then he was beside the suit of armour at the head of the stairs. It gleamed dully, a quite misplaced piece of ostentation; at home they consigned better examples to the cellars. He even doubted, now that he was near, whether the helmet matched the rest.

A grim thought crossed Jago's mind.

It was his duty to look inside the helmet. He reached for the visor and lifted it. Empty! If he was honest with himself, it was a relief. He took his hand away.

The visor dropped back into place with a metallic snap, loud enough to waken anyone in that part of the house. Jago froze momentarily, as though if he moved the whole suit of armour might topple over and clatter nightmarishly down the stairs.

Then he started rapidly back towards his room, floorboards protesting at every step. He reached the door and turned the handle. Too late.

'What in hell is going on?'

D'Estin stood ahead of him in the corridor, naked to the waist.

'I knocked against the armour coming upstairs,' Jago improvised. 'I'm sorry you were disturbed.'

The trainer approached, his head crooked forward menacingly.

'What are you up to, man, moving about the bloody house in the night?'

'I couldn't sleep. I was going for a drink.' It sounded so feeble that he was already thinking of a second excuse.

D'Estin came unpleasantly close and pushed his arm aggressively past Jago's right ear to lean on the door-jamb. The smell of sleep hovered about him.

'You weren't going anywhere else, then?'

'What do you mean?' Jago asked.

'It wouldn't have occurred to your generous and cultivated mind that a certain lady might feel – how shall I put it – desolate and in need of company on a warm summer night?' Sarcasm oozed from D'Estin like the sweat glistening on his chest-hair.

This was unexpected. Jago looked as affronted as a man could in his nightshirt. 'That is a detestable implication, sir! I thoroughly repudiate it! I suggest that you –'

'I suggest,' echoed D'Estin, 'that you were groping in the darkness for the door of her bedroom and knocked against the armour. You wouldn't be the first.'

Jago was genuinely embarrassed. For a moment he actually wished D'Estin had guessed he was searching the house for evidence. That at least would be an honourable charge. Detective work was debasing. Confound it!

He controlled his fury. 'You had better return to bed, D'Estin, before I have this out with you. I shall put these ridiculous insinuations down to your sudden awakening from deep sleep. I apologize for disturbing you.'

In answer, D'Estin jutted his face to within six inches of Jago's and laughed lewdly. His breath was nauseous.

'What is happening?' Isabel's voice, from along the corridor. She was looking out from her room, only her head visible, a long plait dangling beneath it.

D'Estin reacted quickly. 'It's quite all right. You can go back to sleep. I've caught the prowler. He won't be blundering around your door again tonight – unless you invite him, of course.'

Isabel's door slammed.

It was a significant moment in Jago's career. Every instinct urged him to attack D'Estin. Sheer professionalism held him back. For he saw clearly that D'Estin's suggestion, for all its base imputations, gave him a clear excuse for moving furtively about the house at night.

Like a guilty man, he shrugged, sighed and looked at his feet.

Smirking, D'Estin walked away.

Eleven

My dearest Lydia [read Sergeant Cribb],

I do thank you for your letter which reached me yesterday, tho' I must ask that you do not write again. My present choice of occupation is, you will understand, not entirely proper in the eyes of the law, and my advisers here suggest that we should keep my presence at Radstock Hall a closely guarded secret. For the same reason this must be my last letter to you. I am sure I may rely upon you to dispose of it when you have read it.

I am well looked after here, and have never felt so fit in my life. I even have hopes of becoming a celebrity of the ring, as I am now, by default (of a kind which I cannot explain here), the star of this particular school of arms. With luck, and good fist-work, I may soon have sufficient capital to advance my claims with your father.

I was pleased to learn that you have had a communication from Roberta. She, I feel sure, has more of interest to write to you than ever I could. Very little happens here except the daily routine of training.

Be assured that my thoughts are often with you. I shall return *as soon* as I am able.

Until then I remain
Yr. most affectionate
Henry

'What's happened to the Ebony then, Sarge?' Thackeray asked. 'Has he gone the way of Quinton, do you think?'

Cribb was sceptical. 'More likely to have walked out,' he said. 'And if he's done that it must have been for a better offer. Pretty obvious where that came from.'

'Is it, Sarge?' It was obviously not, to everyone.

'The gang that handled Meanix,' Cribb explained with unaccustomed patience. 'Who else could have known where the Ebony was, to say nothing of getting in touch with him? When Meanix kissed the turf it was obvious they needed a new bruiser!'

Thackeray's face lit up. 'Of course!'

'So you can go off sharp to Shoreditch and listen to the chat in the fighting pubs. There's five of 'em, so watch your liquor intake. Johnny Gill's pub, Jane Shore; Mr Parrott's place – the Duke's Head in Norton Folgate; the Sportsman in Boundary Street; the Blue Anchor in Church Street, and the Five Inkhorns in New Nicholl Street. If the Ebony's back in the East End someone there will have wind of it. We can't afford to lose him.'

Long after Thackeray had departed, Cribb sat alone in the office with Jago's letter in front of him, troubling him more than he cared to say.

There was champagne with dinner that evening. Edmund Vibart was unusually sociable; it appeared he had been to London that day and returned in a four-wheeler. He arrived for dinner in a new suit.

'Flash as Newgate Knocker, eh? Not often you see me in nobby-looking clothes, so feast your eyes for once.' He danced across the room to a chair with two wrapped objects on it. 'This is for you, Isabel. The very latest from Maples.'

She unwrapped the parcel.

'Cretonne chintz,' explained Vibart, as she held out the material to examine it. 'You can brighten your rooms with it. And this, D'Estin, is for you. I nearly bought some Eau Figaro – miraculous stuff that restores grey hair to its original colour, what?'

D'Estin, unappreciative, took the object from Vibart and gave it to Isabel to untie for him. It was a revolver.

'Six-shooter, old man. Got it at Holland and Holland's in New Bond Street. You can keep the bloody roughs at bay with it.'

'Thank you.'

'Didn't know what to bring you, Jago, not knowing you so well, but Isabel will tell you what your gift is in a few minutes.'

She, too, was radiant that evening. She wore black silk and diamanté brilliants, the cut of her bodice refuting any suggestion that she was still in mourning. She offered Jago the fruit-bowl.

'Yes. In effect, Henry, you are the most favoured of us all. Edmund has been able to negotiate a contract for you.'

'Really,' said Jago, interested. 'A fight?'

Isabel hesitated a fraction. 'Yes. It will be worth a great deal of money. You can see now why Edmund has taken a premature opportunity to spend some of it.'

'Who is to be my antagonist?'

Nobody answered.

Jago smiled nervously. 'Well, tell me please. Who am I to meet?'

Isabel stood up and came round the table to place a hand on his shoulder. 'You are to meet Sylvanus Morgan.'

'Morgan! The –'

'The Ebony, old man,' confirmed Vibart with an air of total unconcern. 'Don't worry, though. We're not expecting you to win.'

Jago was dazed.

'Allow me to explain, Edmund,' Isabel said. 'But first pour the champagne, Robert, if you please.'

D'Estin, strangely submissive in the last day or two, obeyed.

'Now, Henry,' Isabel continued after resuming her seat. 'Please hear me out before you express any surprise at what I have to tell you. You will know that Sylvanus deserted us quite suddenly and discourteously on Tuesday. Well, it is now quite clear that he had been approached with an offer of higher rewards by a group of men in the East End of London. How they got into contact with him I have yet to discover, but that is another matter. And although I was very angry indeed at his going I later realized that it resolved several difficulties for us.'

'I should bloody say so,' muttered Vibart.

'Our greatest difficulty,' said Isabel, 'was that after the Meanix fight we had no match for Sylvanus. Fist-fighters, as you must be aware, are rare individuals; few men have the courage or physique to earn a living with their knuckles. Oh, there were one or two about – in Birmingham and Manchester – but they weren't in our man's class, you understand, and I do insist that my fighters are not matched below their form. In short, we had nothing to offer Sylvanus, so he left. And as it happens, he went to a man named Matt Beckett, who manages Meanix.'

'Oh,' said Jago, who was beginning to follow the thread.

'Beckett, being a good businessman, saw the possibility of staging a fight between Sylvanus and someone from my school of fighters – a grudge contest, you see, as far as the public are concerned, with Sylvanus determined to defeat the man I choose to replace him.'

'I see.' It was manifestly clear. 'And there is no one but me.'

Isabel laughed. 'Oh, Henry Jago, you do underrate yourself! You are a splendid fist-fighter, with fine prospects. But don't misunderstand me. I am not asking you to defeat Sylvanus.'

Jago was indignant. 'You have made a match for me expecting me to be beaten?'

She clapped her hands. 'That is exactly it, Henry! Now wait one moment! Hear me, please. You are to fight Sylvanus this coming Saturday, and you will lose in the twenty-sixth round.'

'A fixed fight?' protested Jago, on his feet, twenty-two years of decent upbringing rebelling at the prospect.

'If you care to call it that, yes. Now sit down, Henry, and allow me to continue. Sylvanus at this stage of his career cannot afford to lose. One more good mill may earn him a fight with Charlie Mitchell, the best in England. But I am not so insensitive as to suggest that *you* should suffer a defeat. You will fight under another name, and suffer no loss of reputation.'

'My idea,' claimed Vibart proudly. 'And they're paying us three hundred, which isn't bad for a bloody defeat, is it?'

'But I am known here. They saw me fight Judd.'

'The fight will be in Surrey,' explained Isabel, 'and you will take the name of an ex-pugilist – a man we once trained here, who left the country.'

'Who was that?'

D'Estin intervened. 'No small beer, Jago. A game fighter. I'd exchange my moniker for his if I had two good fists.'

'Who was he then?'

'Quinton,' said Isabel. 'Thomas Quinton. You won't have heard of him.'

On the following afternoon Jago was allowed a training run.

Since the arrival of Lydia's letter he had been supervised as rigidly as a workhouse inmate. Today, for some unfathomable reason, D'Estin tossed him a guernsey and told him to put it on and take a run through the grounds for an hour. He went at once.

Once he was sure nobody was following, the sensation of freedom was exhilarating. It was a severely limited freedom, of course; if he tried to escape over the wall he would not get far in conspicuous running-drawers. But there was joy of a kind in simply exercising as one liked, sprinting through glades where sunlight flashed intermittently on one's limbs; stopping to watch a squirrel's acrobatic performance; striking deep into shaded copses where the air was cool as a cellar.

During the run he reviewed the previous night's conversation for perhaps the twelfth time and concluded that there *ought* to be nothing to fear. If the fight with the Ebony was worth three hundred to the loser it was a first-class match. As such it would be the talking-point in every fighting-pub in the East End. Cribb could not fail to hear of it through his numerous contacts. Even if he failed to guess the true identity of the Ebony's opponent he would certainly be there to watch developments. And once he recognized who it was squaring up to the huge Negro he would undoubtedly intervene. Undoubtedly. The sequence of events was all so logical that Jago wondered why he found himself repeatedly going over it in his mind.

He returned to the house soon after three in a pleasant sweat and was met on the front lawn by Isabel carrying a black parasol. His hand felt for his hat in an automatic gesture.

'You look well, Henry. Did you enjoy your run?'

'Certainly, Ma'am. It's a fine afternoon.'

'Are you going to bathe now? You look hot.'

'That was my intention.'

'When you have finished, I must see you. The men representing Sylvanus are coming tonight to make arrangements about the fight. You must be weighed and measured.'

'Is that necessary?' Jago asked dubiously. 'I thought fist-fighters could be matched at any weight.'

She smiled. 'Yes, Henry dear, but the information has to be available for the gambling fraternity and the newspapers. We can use my dressmaker's measure upstairs. When you have bathed, dress as you will for the fight and weigh yourself on the scales in the gymnasium. Then put on a bathrobe and come up to my rooms for measuring. By the look of you, you have added some muscle on your arms and chest in your short stay here.'

Jago took half a step backwards, more confused than embarrassed. Women simply did not make personal remarks or look at men in the way Isabel did. He muttered some acknowledgement and hurried away like a swimmer who had picked the wrong bathing-machine.

An hour later, refreshed but still uncomfortable, Jago stood at the door of Isabel's suite in bathrobe, drawers and canvas pumps. It was ajar, but he knocked.

'That must be you, Henry.' A voice from an inner room.

'Yes. Shall I come back later?'

No chance of that.

'No, silly man! Go into the sitting-room. I shall not keep you waiting long.'

He entered a small, tastefully furnished room, less exotic than he had anticipated. A box of mignonette stood at the centre of a mahogany table. Silhouetted miniatures in two groups hung on the cedarwood panelling. Twin recesses on either side of the hearth were screened by deep blue velvet curtaining.

'Well, then.'

He turned at the sound of her voice and blinked in surprise.

She was wearing white. A white sari.

'Have I startled you, Henry?'

Jago fumbled for words. 'You usually dress in –'

'Black? I wear the colour of mourning, from respect for my late husband. And white is the mourning-colour in the East. In the circumstances, it isn't sacrilegious to wear a white sari, is it? What do you think?'

Jago could only think that Isabel should never wear anything but white. Light was refracted on her neck and the underside of her cheeks, the skin as luminous as porcelain.

'It becomes you.'

She accepted the compliment with the slightest tilt of her eyebrows.

'I bought the material in Regent Street, and had my dressmaker put it together. It probably isn't anything like the authentic Indian dress, but who knows in England? I find it infinitely less constricting than the European fashions.'

A statement he had no difficulty in believing. Isabel crossed the room to draw the curtains from one alcove, and it was evident to Jago's inexpert eye that foundation garments formed no part of Indian fashion.

'This is where I must measure you,' she told him. 'I call it my dressmaking closet. Take off your robe and come over, Henry.'

He obeyed, and when he pushed aside the curtain and stepped into the narrow recess he had an unpleasant shock. Isabel was there with a headless woman. In a moment he realized what it was – a dressmaker's dummy with a dress over it – but the momentary surprise had registered.

'I sometimes startle myself,' Isabel said, smiling. 'She's very lifelike in my new cashmere gown, isn't she? She was fashioned from the measurements of my own figure. Underneath she is just wire and sawdust, poor thing – a terrible disappointment to her admirers, I should think.'

'It's a pretty dress,' ventured Jago, vaguely conscious he was on the brink of a risqué conversation.

'It is ready for the end of my year in mourning,' Isabel said. 'Now will you stand against the vertical measure on that wall please?'

This involved making a narrow passage between Isabel and her headless double. She made no attempt to stand back. He faced the dummy and edged discreetly to the opposite wall. It was only a temporary reprieve from the agony of contact. Isabel was not a short woman, but Jago was over six feet in height. To adjust the sliding arm of the measure above his head she had to stand almost toe to toe with him; from any farther away the attempt would have resulted in loss of balance and the meeting of unthinkable areas of anatomy.

There was no need to ask him to stand straight. He was braced like a guardsman.

'Six feet and half an inch,' she declared at length. 'Sylvanus will not have much advantage in height. What did you weigh?'

'Twelve stone six,' answered Jago.

'Two pounds less than you arrived with. Sylvanus is considerably heavier but that is not all muscle. Now if you will extend your arms I shall measure your reach.' She produced a tape-measure and held one end against his arm-pit. 'Good. If you will keep your arms outstretched I can take your chest measurement.'

Jago had not heard before of fist-fighters being subjected to so comprehensive a physical survey. He tried to relax and submit to science. Somehow two beads of nervous sweat escaped from his right arm-pit and trailed coldly across his ribs.

'Expand your chest Henry.'

She was distractingly close. The air was heavy with her perfume; no English flower he had smelt was anything like it.

'Good. You may have lost a little weight, but you have certainly gained in muscularity. Flex this arm and I will measure the bicep.'

'Will you remember the measurements,' asked Jago with a note of desperation in his voice, 'or should I fetch pencil and paper for you?'

'Thank you, but I have a faultless memory for such things. Your waist, please.'

He felt her bare forearms take the tape behind his back. Monstrous thoughts assailed him. Whatever happened he must keep control. He tried to banish Isabel, sari and scent from his mind. Instead he would concentrate on Sergeant Cribb, that nose and those Piccadilly Weepers.

The potency of Cribb's image lasted for perhaps ten seconds, until Isabel coaxed her tape-measure around Jago's right thigh.

'Is this necessary?' he demanded in an outraged voice.

'Essential,' she murmured, crouching to her task like a boot-boy. 'Just relax, Henry.'

He looked down. The silk drape had slipped from her shoulder, but she had not attempted to replace it. The bodice gaped. With admirable self-control he averted his eyes at once. But as he did so, his thigh twitched involuntarily.

She stood up. 'You really are far too tense, Henry Jago. You are in no state to fight anyone tomorrow night, least of all Sylvanus Morgan. You need massage at once. Come with me.'

There was nothing for it but to follow her as she swept aside the curtain and marched purposefully across the sitting-room and through a door. It was a relief to escape from the unnatural – or too natural – intimacy of the dressmaking closet. On the way he picked up his bathrobe but immediately decided to replace it on the chair; any display of modesty now seemed like weakness.

Jago was in Isabel's bedroom and the door was shut behind him before he had time to collect himself.

'Lie face downwards on the ottoman.'

Not the bed, thank Heaven! He flattened himself to the velvet upholstery like an infantryman on the order of fire. The ottoman was upholstered in crimson and positioned at the foot of a brass double-bed covered with a satin quilt. From his restricted viewpoint he could see a half-open wardrobe with a row of Isabel's boots on the lowest shelf. A mirror on the inside of the door allowed him a glimpse of the dressing-table where she was standing behind him. Its top was crowded with jars, cut-glass bottles and silver-backed brushes. She was pouring some liquid into her cupped hand.

Without another word she came to where he was and sat along the edge with her thigh lightly touching his hip. He felt the mild shock of the cool liquid as she pressed it between his shoulders, and then the warmth of the palms and fingers spreading it across his skin. Her hands worked with a sense of symmetry, distributing the balm evenly, her fingers probing each band of muscle individually, kneading quite forcefully at first, gradually relenting to a stroking movement, until finally the touch was no more than a caress.

Whatever she was using on his body was distinctly aromatic, with a heady muskiness about it, unlike any branded liniment he knew. And it tingled on the skin like champagne on the palate.

'Good. I can feel you relax now. The muscles are becoming more supple.'

Once or twice her fingertips were raised clear of the skin while she continued to massage with the mounts of her palms. Jago found himself waiting for the sensation of her fingers coming consecutively back into contact. It was devilishly hard not to luxuriate. For distraction, he turned his head to look through the vertical bars of the bedstead at the picture over the bed. It was an animal study, but no Landseer. A white stallion, eyes rolling in terror, reared in a desperate attempt to throw a tiger from its back. He would never understand Isabel's taste in art.

He turned elsewhere for inspiration. Every decent influence in his life – parents, two devoted sisters in Gloucestershire, Lydia – dear Lydia, the vicar, his housemaster, Sergeant Cribb – paraded before his troubled conscience, to be ignominiously dismissed. Isabel Vibart dispatched them all with one breath on the nape of his neck.

Her voice was close to his ear. 'Are you comfortable?'

What a question! 'Extremely so.'

'You feel more relaxed here?'

'Quite so.'

'You find it hard to sleep in that room along the corridor?'

Good God! Did she believe D'Estin's ravings the previous night?

'On the contrary. It is an excellent room.'

'That is good. Now I must rest a moment. Massage is tiring work.'

'You do it well.'

'I enjoy it.'

She continued to lean over him. Her hair, which had been swathed in a severe Indian style, must have worked loose with her movements, for he now felt its brushing motion across his shoulders. He arched his back a fraction at the sensation and felt his skin touch warm silk at two points. And as he drew his chest to the velvet again the yielding breasts nestled against his back. His pulse was racing.

'Shall I start again?'

'If you wish to.' He tried to convey the fact that he was not particular about massage any more.

'Then you must allow me to loosen your drawers and slip them over your hips. Otherwise I cannot massage your thighs.'

Fifteen minutes earlier it would have been unthinkable. He felt for the lacing across his stomach.

'That is better. I am used to massaging men, you know.'

He wished she had not said so.

'I must get some more of the embrocation. Anointing oil I like to call it.' She went over to the dressing-table.

He lay with the drawers around his knees and tried not to feel ridiculous. When she returned, she paused, standing at his side to survey him.

'You have a fine back, Henry. Not a mark on you. But I didn't expect to see any.'

'What do you mean?'

'Spike-marks, Henry. You refused the Wrestler's Bridge.'

Her words acted on Jago like a jellyfish-sting in a warm sea. The Wrestler's Bridge! The gym. His humiliation. Now this confirmation that she had indeed been watching D'Estin punish him. Watching from her spy-hole!

His body convulsed with shame. His head twisted to look at her and she knew exactly what was in his mind. There was total contempt in her expression.

Before he could tug his disabling garment about him she fell on his back and with her fingernails clawed it from shoulder to loin.

'There's a mark for you, Casanova!'

Then she fell across the ottoman laughing hideously. Reeling from shame and confusion, Jago quit the room.

Twelve

'That – er – corpse,' said Inspector Jowett with calculated disinterest. 'The one you hooked out of the Thames a week or two ago. Head missing. Didn't you have some theory at the time that he was a prize-fighter?'

'Prize-fighter? Oh yes, prize-fighter. I believe so, sir,' answered Sergeant Cribb, equally restrained. Deprived of the Inspectorial pomp of desk, telephone and bookshelves, Jowett was a mere policeman in plain clothes. Looking down at him as they strolled in Hyde Park, Cribb even doubted whether he came up to the statutory five feet seven. Fancy! Quacks and professors had sought for years for a substance that would add an inch to a man's height. They could have found the secret all the time at Great Scotland Yard – an old school tie.

'You didn't take your investigations any further, then?' Jowett persisted. He had not gone to the trouble of arranging a rendezvous with Cribb to be snubbed like a street salesman.

'I've been very busy, you see, sir,' said Cribb. 'Inquiries don't come singly, as you know. Shall we head over that way, where the crowds are making for?'

Jowett looked in the direction Cribb was indicating. Some two hundred yards away across the grass a gathering of several hundred had formed. He was nervous of crowds. 'What is it – speechmaking? Irishmen? Anarchists?'

'Unlikely, sir,' said Cribb. 'The orators don't stray far from Hyde Park Corner. Might be a prize-fight.'

Jowett rose to the bait. 'Good God! – do you think so? Let's go the other way. We mustn't get involved.'

'Observing them more closely, sir, I'd say it wasn't a prize-fight,' Cribb said. 'Too many of the fair sex for that.' As though that settled the matter, he began walking more briskly towards the centre of interest, with Jowett reluctantly keeping up.

'Last week, Sergeant,' he said, a little breathless, more from anxiety than exercise, 'there was a fist-fight. In Essex.'

'Really, sir?' Inwardly, Cribb flinched. How much did Jowett know?

'Fortunately, it was stopped by the local constable – "an unwelcome blue cloud on the horizon", as the reporter termed him.'

Cribb chuckled. 'Very good, sir.'

'Quite so. Good Lord! What on earth is that?'

Above the level of top-hats and ostrich feathers ahead of them something of great size arched like an elephant struggling to its feet. But this was bright orange in colour, and its shape altered from second to second. It seemed to be straining for freedom.

'A balloon, sir!' said Cribb. 'Must be the French aeronaut they interviewed in the *Morning Post*. He claims it's dirigible. Ovoid in shape, you see, and he carries a propellor on the car. They're inflating it with gas. Capital sight!'

Jowett was not so easily distracted. He stopped, holding Cribb's arm to prevent him going on. 'I didn't arrange for us to meet in secret to watch a blasted balloon-launching. I want to talk to you in private, Cribb. I picked Hyde Park thinking it was inconspicuous.'

'We'd be less conspicuous in a crowd, sir.'

'Possibly, but I need to speak in confidence,' said Jowett. 'Two weeks ago you asked permission to attend prize-fighting. I gave my assent – reluctantly I may say – in the belief that you found attendance there absolutely vital to your investigation.'

'Fundamental, sir.'

'And as I remember I warned you of the possible embarrassment to the Criminal Investigation Department if a County Force learned you had been present at a prize-fight in its area.'

Heavens! What had Jowett found out?

'I don't know whether you were aware when you asked me that attendance – yes, even attendance – at a prize-fight is illegal.'

Already preparing his excuses, Cribb recited the legal precedent. ' "An assembly of persons to witness a prize-fight is an unlawful assembly and everyone present and countenancing the fight is guilty of an offence." Rex versus Billingham, 1826, sir.'

'Thank you. Now, Sergeant, I shall not ask you whether you were present at this squalid affair in Essex, but I think it right

to tell you that if you attend a prize-fight it is your duty to intervene.'

'Yes, sir. I shall.'

Jowett looked up sharply. 'You almost sound as though you
know of one that has been arranged.'

'I –'

'Don't tell me, Sergeant! Simply remember what I have said.
Thugs like those two I read of – Judd and Jago – must be
brought to justice.'

Cribb offered silent thanks for the obtuseness of his superior.
The prospect of one of his staff *attending* a prize-fight was as
awful as anything Jowett was ready to contemplate. Having now
allowed for that possibility he felt able to relax.

'It's the French balloon all right,' he announced confidently.
'Look at the shape. You know, Sergeant, we've got a lot to learn
from across the Channel. Looking ahead – and a policeman
should always have a clear view of the future – I can see excit-
ing possibilities in this ballooning. Imagine a police-balloon
patrolling the air over London. No criminal will feel secure on
the streets.'

Sergeant Cribb was looking ahead, but less far. On the following evening Thomas Quinton, alias Henry Jago, was due to
fight the Ebony. If Thackeray's latest information from Shoreditch were correct, the fight would last twenty-six rounds before
the Negro pole-axed Jago. The fight was arranged for somewhere in Surrey, so everyone but Isabel Vibart would leave
Radstock Hall early, probably by eleven. That woman held the
information he wanted. There should just be time, if he were
ready, to interview her at the Hall, and then set off in pursuit of
the others. He was not notably perturbed by Jowett's instructions, but he did feel under a sentimental obligation to Jago to
stop the fight before the twenty-sixth round if possible.

A cold supper was ordered for that evening, with the intention of getting the servants to their quarters as early as possible.
Consultations about the fixing of fights were best held in total
privacy. For Jago, the informality – one arrived in one's own

time on cold supper evenings – saved an embarrassing confrontation with Isabel. Furthermore, eating alone allowed him time to collect himself before the negotiations. After an early meal he went to his room and did not appear again until the visitors arrived at nine.

They came in a four-wheeler and Jago heard them welcomed by Vibart. Any resentment at the Ebony's desertion had been quite dissolved by the prospect of profit. The bonhomie downstairs was worthy of a Crimea reunion. He went down to join them in the main drawing-room.

'Ah, Jago. You haven't met Matt Beckett.'

It was the strangest sensation shaking hands with a man he had known as a set of notes on a card for nearly two years. *'Beckett, Matthew.'* Hardly a day passed without that name fleetingly impressing itself on his brain. *'Crown tattooed ...'* He found himself checking the details.

Beckett showed no sign of recognizing Jago, although it was not long since they had shared a railway compartment after the Meanix fight. 'You're fit, I hope?' he said with a laugh. 'All we ask of you, mate, is that you can get up when you've been grassed and that you can count to twenty-six, eh, Vibart?'

'No fears on that score,' Vibart assured him. 'Jago's been privately educated.'

'Has he indeed?' Beckett openly sneered. 'Tomorrow night he'll have a new tutor then. Morgan here ain't exactly a university man, but he'll learn you a few points, Jago.'

'You haven't met Mr Foster, Jago,' Vibart intervened. 'He will act as second to Sylvanus tomorrow.'

'Foster, David. Born 1860. Five foot six. Ten stone.' A strong grip for a slight man.

'Pleased to meet you, mate.' That was something for the card. *'Two lower front teeth missing.'*

'Where's Mrs Vibart, then? We ain't got the time for small-talk,' said Beckett. There was menace in his voice, a grey neutrality in his eyes that one could not very well record by Scotland Yard methods.

'She'll be down,' Vibart promised. 'What are you drinking?'

'Rum and shrub for me,' Beckett said. 'You can have ale, Morgan,' he told the Ebony, and added, speaking to Vibart, 'in a pony-glass. We don't want no thick heads tomorrow.'

In spite of his welcome, the Ebony was ill at ease. He received his drink and sat hugely on a small high-backed chair in the centre of the room, concentrating on the pattern of the carpet. Jago selected an armchair against the wall. D'Estin brought him a ginger-beer.

Everyone stood for Isabel's entrance, in a black high-necked dress of surah silk, serene and gracious, difficult to credit as Jago's assailant a few hours earlier. His back still smarted though.

The introductions were made and Beckett at once began stating terms. 'It must seem a fair stand-up fight, with Jago taking the early rounds to shorten the odds. I'll keep Morgan reined until the tenth. You can have first blood. When do you want it?'

'The fourth,' said D'Estin.

'Does he know what to do?'

'You go for the lip,' D'Estin told Jago. 'And as you land, he bites it to make sure and the tide flows. You understand?'

'The fourth,' Jago confirmed, secretly telling himself Cribb would have stopped the fight before then.

'First four knockdowns and first blood to your man, then,' said Becket. 'Then Morgan must win two rounds.'

'Liver-hits,' suggested Foster with relish. 'A man goes down beautiful from a liver-hit. You can always go to work on the face later, Morgan.'

The Ebony nodded. Jago glanced at the black fist enfolding the beer-glass and looked quickly away again.

Isabel spoke: 'We want no permanent injuries. Understand that, Sylvanus. A certain amount of blood is to be expected, but gouging is not. Show me your thumbnails.'

Humbly, the Ebony put out his hands.

'They must be cut. Whatever you do to our man in the final rounds I want him fit to fight again within six months. That means that any cuts must be superficial. What is that dreadful hold when you crook your arm around your adversary's neck and hold his wrist while you batter his face with your free fist?'

'The Suit in Chancery,' the Ebony said.

'You must not use it on Jago.'

'Wait a bit, my lady,' said Beckett. 'Morgan ain't fighting to your orders now. No lasting injuries we agree to, but you can't dictate what punches he throws.'

'Mr Beckett,' said Isabel quietly. 'He is capable of killing a man. Would you be a party to manslaughter?'

Beckett considered the point. Jago, the potential victim, waited for the decision. It occurred to nobody to ask his opinion.

Beckett nodded. 'Very well, then. No Suit in Chancery, Morgan. Now are we agreed on a twenty-six-round fight or would you like Jago to twist his ankle in the fifth and retire?' The sarcasm helped him over the humiliation of conceding a point to Isabel. Plainly he did not like negotiating with a woman.

She ignored him. 'You aren't looking so well as you should, Sylvanus. I hope you are quite fit.'

'Fit enough,' the Ebony said without looking up.

'He'll 'ave Jago on toast in the last rounds,' promised Foster, whose taste for violence seemed unusually well cultivated.

'You gave us no warning when you went,' Isabel continued. 'That was a strange way to treat us after so many months here. It showed a singular lack of gratitude.'

The Ebony lifted his face in surprise. 'Gratitude?'

'Don't blame him, Mrs Vibart,' said Beckett affably. 'Morgan's a professional. He simply accepted a better offer. There ain't many openings for a fist-fighter these days. When one comes you don't turn it down.'

The Ebony, after seeming about to respond, lapsed into silence.

'Shall we settle the financial business here, Mrs Vibart?' Beckett went on. 'I must give you a merry monk, I think.'

'Merry –'

'A monkey,' explained D'Estin. 'Beckett owes you five hundred, Isabel. Two hundred back from your stakes and three hundred for tonight's agreement.'

'Of course. My writing-desk is in the morning-room, Mr Beckett. Perhaps you will come there. I am sure I can leave you gentlemen to arrange the finer details for tomorrow between you. I intend to retire early, so I must wish you all good evening.'

They stood for her. With a rustle of silk she turned, smiled, and was gone, Beckett following. Jago wished she had stayed, and despised himself.

Foster, quite insensitive to the respect Isabel commanded, was quick to comment. 'It ain't every man that goes off with a young widow and five 'undred in flimsies in 'is pocket. We might be taking the four-wheeler back by ourselves tonight, Morgan.'

The remark was unacceptable in any circumstances; spoken by Foster it was odious. Instead of the sly winks he expected he found himself hauled by his shirt-front to within a foot of D'Estin's face.

'I suggest,' the trainer said in no more than a whisper, 'that you retract that remark, because if you don't I shall take the greatest pleasure in returning it to the cess-pit it came from.' The thumb and finger of his mutilated hand were ready to make the attempt.

'I withdraw it,' breathed Foster. 'I apologize.' With that he backed into an armchair and cowered on it like a trapped hare.

D'Estin addressed the Ebony. 'You actually deserted us to rub shoulders with scum like that? There's better company in Colney Hatch.'

The Negro avoided meeting anyone's eyes. His only response was a clenching and unclenching of the fists, more eloquent of helplessness than aggression.

'Just lose one fight and see how they treat you,' D'Estin persisted. 'Don't look to us for help.'

The Ebony got to his feet slowly, looked vacantly at D'Estin, and turned to Vibart. 'I left some things here, in the dressing-room. I'd like to collect them, Mr Vibart. Is the gymnasium open?'

'It should be. If not I'll open it,' Vibart said appeasingly. 'Will you have another drink first?'

'I've had enough already, thank you.'

The Ebony left the room. No one imagined he had anything to collect from the gymnasium. He was driven out by the unendurable atmosphere.

Cigars were exchanged and glasses refilled to revive cordiality. Vibart took the initiative in this. Whenever Isabel was absent he cast his cynicism like a chrysalis and expanded as a personality. 'Sylvanus is bloody worried,' he told Jago, half confidentially. 'You're looking fitter than he expected. Mark my words, he's gone to exercise in the gym!' And then for everyone's ears, brandishing a claret bottle, 'Whatever the Fancy think of tomorrow's set-to, gentlemen, they'll be in no doubt about the quality of the assistance Jago receives. There ain't a more practised bottle-holder than Edmund Vibart in the south of England!'

Beckett, too, was in high spirits when he rejoined them fifteen minutes later, rubbing his hands. 'I'll have a neat whisky now, if you please, Mr Vibart, and drink to the success of our arrangement. Your sister-in-law drives a hard bargain, but I've paid in full and everything's settled. We call you Quinton from now on, Jago –' He stopped suddenly. 'Where's Morgan? Where the hell is Morgan?'

'Collecting some of 'is toggery from the gym,' Foster told him, as if he actually believed it.

'Ah, is that so? Well, he's not necessary to our last item of business. The time and place, gentlemen, the time and place. Now let's say this at the outset. We want no trouble from the police. They've queered too many pitches in the last year or two by getting wind of a fight before it takes place. So I've made it known that we've settled on Surrey and I hope it's reached the law's ears, for now I'd like to propose that we set up stakes in Kent – out Tunbridge Wells way. There's a fast train out from London Bridge at noon. We can put up there for a handsome lunch and then hire ourselves some swell carriages and pairs to take us into the country in style. Then Jago here – sorry, Quinton – and Morgan can have their good old-fashioned mill with the raw 'uns, while half the blues in Surrey are wearing out shoe-leather looking for 'em.'

'It sounds a capital arrangement to me,' said Vibart enthusiastically.

Jago was thinking of Sergeant Cribb. 'What about the onlookers – the Fancy and the bookies? How will they know we're not contesting the fight in Surrey?'

'They won't – until about eleven tomorrow morning, when I let slip the word,' Beckett explained. 'That's early enough for the needle-pointed division. Every fighting-pub in the East End will know within the hour. Are we agreed, then?'

'Entirely,' said Vibart after a nod from D'Estin.

Beckett stood, holding his glass high. 'A toast to twenty-six sledge-hammering rounds at Tunbridge Wells, then.'

Jago sipped at his ginger-beer, somewhat relieved that the Ebony had not been there to hear the toast. In fact it was some ten minutes before Sylvanus did return, and then he confounded everyone by having with him a bundle wrapped in a bathrobe that Jago remembered seeing in the gym.

'What have you got there, Morgan – Mrs Vibart's silver collection?' quipped Beckett. 'We'd better get you away, man, before they loose the dogs on you. He's scared of your dogs, you know, Vibart. He wouldn't think of leaving Radstock Hall by night.'

'He's wise,' said Vibart. 'But don't concern yourselves gentlemen. While the gates are open, as they are tonight, we keep the dogs locked up. When your carriage has left I shall unleash them. In fact, I should be grateful to join you as far as the gate.'

Outside, the warmth of the day lingered, although it was approaching eleven. The four men settled themselves in the carriage, Foster taking the reins.

'Remember, Jago,' Beckett called through the darkness. 'Twenty-five times you come to scratch. Leave the rest to Morgan.'

Foster laughed uproariously and cracked the whip. Long after the shape of the carriage was lost against the trees his cackles could be heard above the grating wheels.

D'Estin nudged Jago's arm. 'Nervous? Let's have a game of billiards. You'll sleep all the better for it.'

Thirteen

D'Estin was right. Retiring shortly before midnight, Jago
settled quickly into untroubled sleep and woke much refreshed
to sunshine and the colloquy of the rook community on his side
of the house: no melodious awakening, but preferable to the
squeak and trundle of hand-carts and carriage wheels outside his
lodgings at Palace Place. There had always been a rookery at
home, at Chapeldurham; with his eyes trained on the ceiling it
was amusing how graphically the carving revived early memories.
Each one in a line of three nannies was available for recall with
her distinctive morning ritual: cold bath with coal-tar soap;
wrestling-match under the quilt; and rhubarb pills and stretching exercises.

He had been fully awake for perhaps three minutes when the
second sound invaded his consciousness. It had not been there
on other mornings – a persistent ululation, drowned at times by
the clamour from the rooks, but continuing at its own level. A
sound uncharacteristic of any bird or animal he knew, but certainly not of human origin. If only their racket would stop for a
minute he might distinguish some recognizable cadence. In
exasperation he threw back the bedding, walked to the window
and pulled up the lower casement. Then he leaned out to catch
the sound more acutely.

The source was clear at once. Some forty yards to his left, on
the lawn adjacent to the billiard-room and the gymnasium
wing, were two huge dogs, Irish wolfhounds, the nocturnal
guards of Radstock Hall. They stood facing the main block,
rooted apparently to one small area of lawn, sometimes backing
a few steps and then recovering the ground, straining to lift their
muzzles to the maximum elevation, and all the time maintaining
a series of melancholy howls that combined to make the weird
monotone Jago had heard. He watched them in mystification;
this was no part of their routine. Once or twice each night he
would hear them baying as they patrolled the woods, but by

dawn they always returned to the lodge, waiting to be re-admitted and fed.

One of the dogs appeared to have seen Jago, for it turned to direct its howling at him. But it made no attempt to approach. The small area of grass which they chose to regard as their pound was clearly defined by their prints in the dew; they must have been there for an hour at least. Yet there was nothing within the patch that he could see – no dead rabbit or resisting hedgehog – to detain them. In its agitation one of the dogs began rearing on its hind legs, and it was then Jago realized their howls were directed at an upper window of the house, the fourth away from his: Isabel's.

He came away from the window, drawing it down to deaden the sound and allow him to consider what to do. Dogs were not rational creatures and it was possible that their alarming behaviour was due to some trick of light or scent, or that some canine disorder had affected them. They were trained guard-dogs, however, and it could be that they had trailed a genuine scent to the point where they could no longer follow. Some intruder might have scaled the drainpipes under Isabel's window.

Jago felt bound to check that she was safe. He decided to rouse Vibart; it would certainly not do to intrude on Isabel alone. Both Vibart and D'Estin slept in rooms on the south side of the house and could not possibly have seen the dogs, even if they had dimly heard them. He drew on his bathrobe and went quickly along the corridor past D'Estin's door to Vibart's room.

Vibart must have been deeply asleep. He came to the door at the fourth burst of knocking, slit-eyed and tousled.

'You? What in God's name do you want at this confounded hour?'

'I think someone may have broken in.'

'Broken in? Burglar you mean?'

'I don't know,' said Jago. 'The dogs –'

'The bloody dogs!' exclaimed Vibart, his lower lip jutting forward in annoyance. 'You come disturbing me because the bloody dogs are barking? Listen to me, Jago. If there *is* a damned burglar in the house, which I doubt, he won't set foot outside it while those brutes are loose, so you can go back to bed and let him sweat it out downstairs or wherever he is till morning. If you want to apprehend him you can do it on your own. You're trained to look after yourself, aren't you?'

He was. He was also trained to cope with uncooperative members of the public. As Vibart drew back and slammed the door Jago put his foot in the way. It was done so automatically that he forgot he was wearing neither shoes nor socks.

To his credit he made only a muted yell of pain, and the rest of the house slept on while he executed an impromptu *entrechat*. It was sufficient to hold Vibart's attention while the initial pain subsided.

'Isabel,' Jago finally managed to say. 'The dogs are barking outside her window. I think we should see that she's all right.'

Without another word Vibart took down a dressing-gown from the back of the door and led Jago along the corridor to Isabel's suite. In that part of the house the noise made by the dogs was quite audible. It seemed inconceivable that she had not been disturbed by them herself.

Vibart knocked.

They waited.

A second knock.

'Possibly she can't hear us knocking from the bedroom,' Jago suggested.

Vibart turned the handle and they went into the first room of the suite, the sitting-room. It was in perfect order.

'Isabel!' Vibart called. The plaint of the dogs must have drowned any reply. He knocked twice on the closed door of her bedroom. 'Isabel!'

No reply.

He turned the handle of the door and peered in. Jago stood back.

From Vibart's throat came a low moan, almost matching the chorus of the dogs. He closed the door, his face ashen.

'What is it?' said Jago.

Vibart lurched to a chair. With a movement of the head he indicated that Jago should look for himself.

132

He opened the door.

The section of the room opposite the casement window was lit by the near-silver sun, low-angled behind the elms outside. So before the total scene could make an impression the eye was fixed by details, surfaces of cut-glass and mother-of-pearl – powder jars and hair brushes on the dressing-table – that scintillated through the full range of the spectrum. The brass-work of the bedstead, too, was highlighted, so that it required a conscious focal effort to look beyond it to the dazzling ocean of bed-linen and the island of almost dry blood in which Isabel Vibart lay.

Death had deprived her of one kind of beauty, but invested her with another. She lay across the sheets obliquely in a white-embroidered night-chemise torn from collar to waist, revealing a cluster of stab-wounds in the region of the heart. They had bled heavily. Without its vanities, jewellery, hairpins, corsets, all-enveloping dress, her body was graced by a naturalness Jago had never seen in a woman. The pure sunlight glowing on the statuesque limbs – why ever did such beauty have to be concealed through life? – banished even the suggestion of immodesty. Her deep-brown hair, loose and luxuriant, was drawn from her face to trail over the edge of the bed so that its ends touched the carpet. Near that point on the floor was a white peignoir trimmed with lace and ribbons. The murderer had used it to wipe the excess of blood from his hands and knife.

Jago felt himself trembling; whether from shock or anger he did not know. Neither reaction was desirable in a policeman, and his training urged him to approach this situation professionally. But could one even begin to treat this as a 'case', a set of circumstances to be analysed on deductive principles? His personal involvement, his revulsion at such violence, held him absolutely. Isabel was murdered, and until his brain could absorb that stupefying fact, it was no good playing at being a detective.

Vibart, re-entering the bedroom from behind Jago, broke through his reverie. 'You can see why he did this.'

He was pointing to the open door of a small safe, set in

the wall to their right. It was empty. The key was still in the lock.

'The money,' Vibart explained. 'Beckett handed her five hundred pounds last night. Five hundred! What a price for Isabel's life!'

'What do you mean?' Jago asked. 'Are you saying you know who did this?'

'Isn't it obvious? Morgan killed her. He hated her anyway, but he killed her for the money. He was out of the room last night for half an hour or more. Didn't you see the bundle he brought back afterwards? There must have been blood on his clothes and hands. He wore the dressing gown to kill her and carried it away with him afterwards. Knife, money, bloodstained hands – they were all hidden in that bundle.'

Jago's faculties were beginning now to function professionally. The situation, he realized, placed him in an appalling dilemma. He could admit at once to being a policeman and take command until a senior officer could be fetched; but that could expose and destroy Cribb's entire investigation into the dead pugilists. Or he could continue in his masquerade, possibly gaining privileged information as the others reacted to the new circumstances; that, he well knew, might lead to an unanswerable investigation into his conduct as an officer. For the present, he would delay the decision.

'We must tell D'Estin,' he said. 'Then one of us should go for the police.'

'The police?' repeated Vibart in disbelief. 'You must be mad! Do you think they can help her now, coming here to turn the blasted place upside down and bring us all into court?'

'I wasn't thinking,' said Jago. 'Those dogs outside – I can't concentrate for their howling. Can you get them away from the house? I'll rouse D'Estin.' He would gain time, perhaps fifteen minutes, while Vibart returned them to the lodge. Before he went to D'Estin he would examine the room alone; that was exactly what he would do if he were a uniformed investigator.

'Very well,' said Vibart. 'What got them into this state, do you think?'

'The smell of blood,' said Jago. 'An open window. Warm sun. Any hunting dog would have got the scent. Take them away at once, can't you?'

'I'll get some clothes on,' Vibart agreed and went off to his room.

In his role as sleuth Jago approached the bed and touched the largest bloodstain. It was practically dry. Controlling his emotions now, he bent to examine the stab-wounds. He was no expert, but they told him the murder weapon was broad-bladed, and had been thrust into the flesh with great force five times. There was also bruising on the throat and left shoulder, suggesting she had been held down by the non-striking hand. Her hands were unmarked, the fingernails unbroken; she had not had a chance to fight.

He looked around the room. The silk dress she had worn the previous evening was hanging on the side of the wardrobe, the folds arranged to prevent creasing. On a painted satinwood chair nearby the other garments had been put to air, the underskirt draped across the arms, the corset, black like the rest, over the back. The stockings and garters lay unseparated near the boots on the floor, but it was clear enough from the arrangement of the rest that Isabel had not been disturbed before getting into bed. Nor had she got up to admit her murderer; even a woman as unreserved as she would have put her undergarments out of sight first.

He crossed to the safe. It was a small metal container, certainly large enough to have held a hundred five-pound notes. Earlier he would have dearly liked to examine its contents for the evidence Cribb required. Now it was quite empty.

Suddenly Jago turned in surprise. From outside, under the window, had come two reports. He darted to the sill and looked out. The two dogs lay motionless on the lawn. Presently Vibart, carrying a gun, approached their great bodies with caution, holding it ready for a third shot.

'Why in God's name did you do that?' Jago shouted down. He was incensed. Hadn't there been enough meaningless violence already?

Vibart gave no answer until he was satisfied, by shifting the fallen bodies with his foot, that they were really dead.

'They were hers,' he shouted back. 'There's no sense in keeping them on now. They didn't save her from Morgan, did they? Useless brutes. Better off dead.'

A movement behind Jago made him turn. D'Estin had entered the room and was standing facing the bed, shaking his head in incomprehension.

'I heard shooting,' he said. 'But this . . .'

'I was coming to tell you,' Jago said. 'Vibart and I found her a few minutes ago. He's outside. He just shot the dogs with that gun he bought you. He must have woken the entire household.'

'We must stop the servants finding out about this,' said D'Estin, collecting himself. 'We want no questions – police – that sort of thing. We'll settle the score in our own way. They emptied the safe, did they? One of those bastards who came last night did this. It was more than they could bear to part with five hundred, even when they stood to gain twice as much in the fight.' He came to the window. 'What's that idiot going to do with the dogs?' He leaned out and shouted to Vibart. 'Move them into the woodshed, man! We want no questions about this.'

'It must be six-thirty by now,' said Jago. 'What time does Mrs Gruber come to wake her?'

'Quarter to eight. She'll be down in the kitchens by now. Must have heard that halfwit shooting. He'll have to tell her he was after game. Look, I'd better get the servants out of the way altogether. I'll go down there now and tell 'em Isabel went off to London last night, and we're off shortly, so that they can all take the week-end off.'

'That will sound very sudden,' cautioned Jago.

'You didn't know Isabel. She was as liable to give them a day off at the drop of a hat as she was to keep 'em working hours after their time. They won't think anything of it.'

'You ought to dress first then. There is time.'

D'Estin nodded, and left. Jago became a policeman again and turned to the window to examine the sill. There was no sign of anyone having entered that way. As the pipes outside were arranged, the climb looked a more difficult feat than he had thought at first. The six feet of brickwork to be bridged between pipe and window was cleared of ivy and had no obvious footholds. Besides, the dogs would certainly have attacked anyone in the grounds at night. Vibart's supposition that the Ebony was responsible and had taken all the evidence away in the four-wheeler seemed the best explanation. Certainly the Negro had no regard for Isabel; anyone could see the simmering scorn in his eyes whenever she had spoken patronizingly to him.

Vibart returned from depositing the dogs' bodies in the wood-shed. 'The servants are bloody delighted! D'Estin's given them the weekend off. I say, shouldn't we draw the curtains or something?'

Jago did so. Then, between them, they lifted Isabel's body to a more restful position on the bed and covered it with a clean sheet which Vibart fetched from the linen-store in the window-seat on the landing.

After a few minutes they were joined in the dressing-room adjacent by D'Estin. Nobody had suggested a conference, but by tacit consent they seated themselves there, and Vibart summarized the position.

'I think we are agreed that only one man can be responsible for this appalling deed, and that is Morgan. He left us last night after Isabel had gone to bed, and he was gone for three-quarters of a bloody hour looking for a few clothes in the gym. He knew she had the money by then and he knew where her room was. Probably he did pick up the dressing-gown from the gym and then wore it to protect his clothes as he stabbed her. When it was done he wiped his hands on the night-jacket in there and then made a bundle of the dressing-gown with the knife and money inside it.'

'And he thinks he's clear because, whatever we suspect, we wouldn't be fools enough to bring in the police,' added D'Estin.

Jago nodded, allowing others to draw conclusions.

'But the bastard's made a mistake if he thinks that's the last he's heard of the matter,' continued D'Estin. 'I don't know if I speak for you two as well, but I certainly plan to settle the score.'

'I'm with you,' said Vibart at once.

'What can we do?' said Jago without committing himself.

'Nothing till we know where he is,' said D'Estin. 'Our only chance of catching up with him is to go through with the fight as planned. Afterwards we can get him away and give him a taste of our kind of justice.'

Vibart lit a cigar. He was ready for a long debate on strategy. 'Surely Beckett will have him carefully protected. He may have been a party to this murder himself.'

'That's possible,' D'Estin agreed. 'But once Beckett has his hands on the money he won't be bothered about his ebony friend. We simply go to the nearest pub with them, as you always do after a fight, and wait our chance to move Morgan out. After twenty-six rounds with Jago here he won't be in much of a state to argue.'

Jago smiled feebly.

'Shall we knife him?' asked Vibart matter-of-factly.

'Shooting's cleaner. I've got the revolver. We'll dump him in the nearest river. Are you with us, Jago? It means you go through with the fight as it was arranged last night. It won't be all lavender fighting a man you know to be a bloody murderer. Are you game?'

Now was hardly the time to admit oneself on the side of the law.

'Game? Never more so,' declared Jago earnestly.

Fourteen

'I wouldn't do that, Thackeray,' said Sergeant Cribb unexpectedly.

'Do what, Sarge?'

'Lie on your back in the grass.'

Thackeray propped himself on to one elbow and squinted at Cribb. 'Why?'

'Grasshoppers.'

'*Grasshoppers*, Sarge? What do you mean?'

Cribb paused a second, dissecting a dandelion. 'Poor-sighted little parties, grasshoppers.'

Thackeray's eyes gaped.

'If one of 'em sees that crop turned skywards,' continued Cribb, eyeing the six-day stubble on Thackeray's chin, 'he's liable to make a jump for it and end up in your mouth.'

There were times, even in the country under a cloudless sky at the height of summer, when Thackeray understood what drove men to violent crime. Without a word, he slumped down again.

Two and a half hours they had lain there in the long grass like scouts on the North-West Frontier, Cribb periodically training his field-glasses on the Hall. All the action had taken place in the first half-hour. Two women in their forties and an elderly man had passed within thirty yards of them on their way to the gate. From their dress they were obviously of the servant class, the man probably a gardener and the women cooks or maidservants. They chatted excitedly and with obvious pleasure.

'Day off for them,' decided Cribb. 'Even the old 'un looks as corky as a two-year-old.'

After that, though, nothing for two hours. Small wonder that Thackeray finally turned on his back. The day had started for him at six, a mortifying hour for a senior constable to be afoot, with Blackfriars Road still wet from the water-cart, and a full two hours to go before the dossers got turned out of the Salvation Army shelter. Then a far from comfortable third-class journey out to Rainham on the London and Southend and an hour's walk in the sun to Radstock Hall. After footing it last time through rain and mud he had brought his Inverness and heaviest boots and now regretted it. He had blisters the size of pennies, he was sure, but dared not examine them for fear of the feet swelling and never going back into the boots. He closed his eyes and imagined himself checking closing-time in Hampstead.

'Here they come,' said Cribb. 'Take a look while I check my watch.'

Thackeray turned over at once and peered through the field-glasses. He saw Vibart waiting in the gig at the front of the Hall, whip in hand, while Jago and D'Estin manhandled a portmanteau aboard.

'Eleven,' said Cribb. 'Just as I expected.'

'Then, why,' pondered Thackeray, 'did you drag me across the fields blowing like a confounded grampus at eight-thirty?' He trained the glasses on the one constable in the Force he would not have changed places with at that moment. Jago was now seated in the gig; from the set of his shoulders it might well have been a tumbril. D'Estin climbed up to join him and Vibart shook the reins.

'Pity we can't give him a wave to let him know we're here,' said Thackeray, in a surge of sympathy, as the trap approached along the drive.

Cribb sniffed. 'That's the sure way to give him apoplexy. Jago's expecting to see us waiting at the ringside, not here.'

'Shouldn't we follow then, Sarge?' urged Thackeray as the carriage trundled past, gathering speed. 'He won't thank us for arriving late. Suppose we lost them altogether.'

'No fear of that. They'll be taking the eleven-forty to Fenchurch Street and then cabbing across to London Bridge. There'll be a pretty conspicuous contingent of the Fancy waiting to travel out to Surrey with 'em. Won't need much detective-work to find out which train they all boarded.'

That was not Thackeray's point. 'But they could start the fight before we get there.'

'Probably will,' agreed Cribb nonchalantly. 'We've more important business on hand than sparing Jago a few rounds in a prize-ring.'

'He might be maimed for life!' protested Thackeray, appalled at such callousness. Had Cribb forgotten the state of the Stepney Ox after the Ebony had dealt with him?

'Not very likely,' the Sergeant retorted, getting to his feet and clapping the field-glasses back into their case. 'Don't forget

Jago's had a week's paid instruction in self-defence from a professor in the art. Fellow should be able to look after himself. Besides, the Ebony won't want to fell him too early. We'll do our best to get there before the claret flows. If we don't, the Yard will foot the doctor's bills.'

With that touching assurance Cribb marched decisively to the drive-way and headed towards the front entrance of Radstock Hall. Thackeray, shaking his head in disbelief, picked up his cape and bowler and followed.

When the sergeant's repeated knocking and ringing brought no response he stood sceptically scratching his side-whiskers.

'Why doesn't the pesky woman come?' he said aloud, backing away from the door to look for signs of life at the windows.

Thackeray remained silent. He knew Cribb's moods too well to venture any suggestion.

The sergeant gave one more tug at the bell, frustrated as any front-door pedlar. Then he stalked huffily across the lawns towards the back of the building, Thackeray ambling behind. While Cribb tried the kitchen door, his assistant decided to examine the woodshed. It was fastened by a simple latch, which yielded easily.

Thackeray gave a long, low whistle. Cribb turned from the lock he was struggling inexpertly to ease open with a piece of wire.

'What is it?'

'Dogs, Sarge. Two ruddy great wolf-hounds with bullets through their brains.'

Cribb went to see for himself. The bodies lay just inside the door across the threshold, as though they were too heavy to drag any further into the hut. No attempt had been made to cover them.

'Not long dead,' said Cribb. 'Why should anyone do that?'

'Could be that Mrs Vibart has quit Radstock Hall for a while, and they've no further use for the guard-dogs,' ventured Thackeray. 'It's a savage way to treat dumb animals, but these people ain't over-sentimental.'

'We'll break into the house,' decided Cribb. He stepped

across the bodies and picked up a short stump of wood. The subtle art of springing locks with wire could be practised some other time. He returned to the kitchen area and selected a window. Then he shattered the glass and felt for the catch. Opened, the window was wide enough to admit a slim man. Thackeray looked on dubiously.

'I'd better make a back for you, Sarge.'

A steady and substantial back. Cribb stepped from it through the window into the kitchen and unlocked the door to admit Thackeray. 'You're probably right,' he told the constable. 'It's ten to one now that there isn't a living soul in the house, but we'd better announce ourselves just the same. And take off your hat.' He passed from the kitchen along a short passage to the entrance hall. 'Looks as central a place as any,' he said, and then cupped his hands to his mouth and shouted, 'Hello there! Mrs Vibart! Hello! Is anyone there?'

The words must certainly have been heard through the building. The two intruders waited while the resonance died away.

'Theory confirmed, then,' said Cribb. 'An empty house.' He took out the watch from his waistcoat. 'That gives us almost an hour to find the evidence I want before we need to get off to London. Papers, mainly – contracts, diaries, training programmes – anything to prove Quinton was here. I'll take the rooms downstairs and you can go up. Try all the bedrooms. It's unlikely they've left any of his clothes in a room, but we can't neglect the possibility.'

Cribb began downstairs by opening all the doors in sight, found the morning-room, and went straight to the writing-desk. It was locked, a handsome piece of furniture, a satinwood davenport banded with rosewood, which Cribb without hesitation splintered at the lock with a paper-knife. He need not have bothered; it contained a dozen or so sheets of paper, ink and a few sachet-cards. The side-drawers at first promised more. One yielded a large bound account book. He opened it on the desk lid and began thumbing through the pages. If there was evidence there, it was going to take time to find. On a first inspection the accounts seemed restricted to house-keeping expenses and servants' wages. He delved into the lower drawer, but there were only ancient copies of *The Times* in there. Not even a sporting paper.

'Sergeant!' Thackeray's sudden shout was unusually urgent.

Cribb left the desk as it was and ran to the staircase, mounting it in threes.

'In here!' The constable was at a door at the top of the stairs. Cribb followed him through a dressing-room to a second door. 'It was locked,' Thackeray explained, 'so I put my boot to it.' The splintered door frame showed the result.

Cribb walked to the bed and gently peeled back the sheet from Isabel Vibart's body. It was unclothed, and blood had been washed from the wounds below the left breast, ugly stab-wounds, all the more offensive for being cleaned and exposed as gaping punctures in the otherwise flawless flesh. After carefully examining the bruised neck and left shoulder and the hands and fingernails Cribb replaced the sheet without a word.

Thackeray waited, his brain in a ferment of questions he dared not put to Cribb. Who would want to stab Isabel Vibart, if this were she? How long had she been dead? Who had cleaned her wounds? Why were the servants in such high spirits when they left the Hall? What had this to do with the shot dogs? Or the death of Quinton?

Cribb's reaction began at a more practical level. 'Whoever did this had a rare amount of blood on his clothes.' His eyes lighted on a linen-basket in the corner of the room. 'Take a look in there.'

Thackeray drew out a pair of heavily bloodstained sheets and spread them across the floor for Cribb to examine. They manifestly confirmed the Sergeant's deduction. He turned to look at the still-open safe in the wall.

'Theft?' murmured Thackeray, as he replaced the sheets in the basket.

'Could be.' Cribb was already at the window, examining the sill. 'But the murderer came through the door in my opinion.' He tapped his nose with his forefinger as though it might lead him independently to the vital clue. Then he surprised Thackeray. 'She was a very handsome woman, and I'm sorry she was knifed, but she's likely to distract us at the moment. It's Quinton's murderer I need to find. If Jago's half the detective he ought to be *he'll* know who murdered Mrs Vibart. We've barely twenty minutes now, Thackeray. Carry on the search for evidence of Thomas Quinton.'

Really! With a scarcely veiled shrug of the shoulders, Thackeray went off to search the other bedrooms. If he found a corpse in each one he doubted whether it would impress Cribb in his present mood. He heard him return downstairs.

It was methodical, Thackeray reasoned, to go to the farthest room first and work back towards the staircase, so he followed the corridor as far as he could and opened the door facing him, not without a discreet knock. Rarely had he seen such disorder in a respectable house; he might have stepped into a common lodging-house in H Division. An unmade bed was piled with newspapers and sheets of music. The Canterbury which should have held the music, a fine papier-mâché rack inlaid with mother-of-pearl, was empty and upside down on the washstand, among shaving mugs and empty wine bottles. Thackeray stepped into the room, taking care not to crush a china dog lying in his path, but denting a copper kettle with his other foot. Scarcely a foot of flooring was not occupied by discarded clothes or ornaments ousted from the mantelpiece. The drawers, when he examined them, were practically empty; all the clothes, he supposed, were scattered about the room. Even the organ – a deuced eccentric item of furniture for a bedroom, but supposedly the occupant was a devoted musician – served as a coat-hanger, for a nightshirt was suspended on one candle-holder and a tall hat on the other. He pulled open the hinged doors at the front and peered into the mechanism. Pianos had been known to harbour vital evidence on occasions; why not organs? This one, though, had nothing more sinister than dust and dead flies. Thackeray brushed his sleeve, took a last look in the wardrobe, and abandoned the room.

He moved to the next, D'Estin's, by the size of the suits in the wardrobe. By contrast, exceedingly tidy – fit for an officer's inspection. He had to search to find any personal items other than clothes. On top of the chest of drawers was a gun-case, empty. The case of butterflies on the mantelpiece had long lost its ornamental quality; as he moved it to look behind, a fritillary and its pin dropped to join the other casualties at the bottom of the case. He gave his attention to the suits, feeling (with a slight twinge of shame) into the pockets for letters. They contained nothing but handkerchiefs and small change. D'Estin was either singularly careful or totally friendless.

The next bedroom had obviously been unused, so after a cursory search Thackeray moved on to one which had certainly been slept in. The bedclothes were still flung back, and would remain so now that the servants had gone away. Under the bed was a portmanteau, which he dragged out in some expectation. He soon unfastened the straps and pulled back the lid. There was a framed picture inside, face downwards. Quinton? He turned it over. Blondin. He was in Henry Jago's room.

Thackeray was never sure afterwards why he felt an impulse when he got up from his knees to lift the pillow of Jago's bed. But he remembered for the rest of his career the shock of discovering there a large bundle of five-pound notes. There must have been a hundred on the mattress, loosely tied with string. A hundred fivers! Jago, he knew, came from a well-to-do family, but how could he possibly have taken so much to Radstock Hall? And why? It was equivalent to six years' pay! He dropped the pillow.

'Sergeant!'

Cribb came up like a surfacing dolphin. 'Found something?'

Gingerly, Thackeray lifted the edge of the pillow again, ready to admit to hallucination. The bundle remained there. He almost whispered, 'Jago.' For the present he was stunned by the monstrous implications.

Cribb picked up the notes and riffled the edges speculatively across his palm. Then he put them in his pocket. 'Precious little time,' he said. 'Better look at the next room.'

Thackeray gladly went, tacitly agreeing that, whatever his discovery meant, there were dangers in trying to account for it.

If corruption were involved, it was as contagious as cholera. When three Chief-Inspectors could be brought to trial, what were the chances of a sergeant and two constables?

Ten minutes later he sat glumly on the window-seat at the head of the stairs with Cribb, having found none of the evidence they needed.

'It's in this place somewhere,' Cribb said, 'and all together. I've done every deuced room downstairs, including the servants' quarters. Even felt the panelling in the hall. These old buildings –' He broke off and galloped downstairs, watched in amazement by Thackeray. Then he commenced reclimbing the stairs on his hands and knees, tapping each one. 'Should have thought of it,' he shouted up as he worked. 'Tudor building. Priest's hole. There was a Catholic priest who spent his life touring the country constructing the things. They'd use the roof as a chapel and have a hiding-place for the priest close by. Usually in the stairs.' He tapped at the wood with increasing agitation as he neared the top of the stairs. They sounded consistently solid. He reached the last stair, thumped at it like a bailiff, and then straightened up, more surprised than disappointed. 'Set of blasted Protestants,' he said, as he sat with Thackeray again, surveying his reddened knuckles.

He withdrew his watch, studied it, and shook his head.

'Can you ride a horse?' he asked unexpectedly.

'A horse? I've sat in a saddle once or twice, Sarge, but I can't claim to have much experience.'

'Must be a pair of hacks in the stables,' Cribb explained. 'You remember D'Estin and company riding out to the Meanix fight?'

Like a scene from his childhood. 'Certainly, Sarge.'

'We can give ourselves another twenty minutes, then.'

Thackeray said nothing. Personally he doubted whether twenty minutes more at Radstock Hall were worth saddle-soreness for a week. He put his hands on the edge of the window-seat to raise himself for a further search, although he did not know where. As he did so, there was a sound from inside, a dull thud.

'Did you look in here?' demanded Cribb.

Thackeray nodded. Of course he had. Wasn't it an obvious place? 'Just bedding, Sergeant. Sheets and pillow-cases. I lifted them all out. There's nothing else in there.'

'I believe you,' said Cribb. All the same, he pulled back the hasp that secured the lid of the window-seat and lifted it.

There was nothing inside.

Thackeray blinked. 'It's impossible! There were sheets –'

'False bottom.' Cribb was already on his knees groping at the sides of the interior for a release catch. 'It opened up and they slid underneath.'

But in spite of his methodical probing of the sides and bottom, the trick would not work for Cribb. The chest, which was about five feet in length, two feet wide and the same in depth, was built of solid oak. It would not be easy to smash one's way through.

'Give me your hat.'

Mystified, Thackeray handed over his bowler. Cribb dropped it into the window-seat and closed the lid. Then he opened it. The hat was still there.

'Blast!'

He slammed the lid down again, and lifted it a second time. There was the hat.

'When you got up,' Cribb said, 'you must have set the thing in motion. That was when we heard it. Sit down again.'

Thackeray obeyed.

'Now get up.'

Thackeray put his hands along the edge to pull his considerable weight forward and upward. But when he rose and the lid was lifted the hat remained obstinately in position like a cat by the milk-cart.

'I think I know what it was, Sarge,' said Thackeray on a sudden inspiration. 'Close the lid.'

Cribb did so, and the constable then began feeling and pressing the brass hasp. After a moment there was a distinct movement from inside.

'I felt it go, Sarge!' he said in excitement. 'You turn the staple to the right.' He lifted the lid and confirmed that the hat had

147

actually vanished. Then he tried manipulating the hasp again. 'It won't work unless the lid is closed.'

'Get inside, then,' Cribb ordered without hesitation. 'Wedge something against the bottom when I try to force the lid open again.'

Thackeray climbed in, feeling like the passive partner in a music-hall turn. It was not easy wedging a six-foot frame into a space designed for five. The lid came down. He waited in the darkness, uncertain what to expect, while Cribb fiddled with the hasp on the outside. The air was musty.

Cribb lifted the lid. 'It won't turn. Can you force your feet against the end and take your weight off the floor?'

In darkness again, Thackeray braced against the sides to suspend himself clear of the floor. To a muffled shout of triumph from outside, it swung downwards beneath him. He lowered one foot into the cavity. Three feet down it touched something dome-shaped. His hat.

'Are you all right?' called Cribb.

'Yes, Sarge. I'm standing in the lower part now, but I can't see what size it is.'

'Take off your boots and wedge them against the base to stop it closing when I force open the lid.'

He did so, crouching clear of the hinging mechanism. 'All right, now!'

An inch-wide strip of daylight severed the blackness above him. He leaned on the hinged base as Cribb strained to widen the gap. After a moment the combined force of the two men overcame the work of the Tudor carpenter. To the sound of splintering wood, the lid swung back. Thackeray stood upright inside with his face at the level of the lid.

'What's inside, then?' Cribb demanded.

Thackeray crouched and retrieved his crushed bowler hat and a set of pillow-cases and handed them to the sergeant. He bent again. 'There's something else.'

It was an overcoat, an ulster, heavily stained with blood. Some stains were old, some fresh enough to be still slightly damp.

Cribb felt the coat pockets and took out a long straight-bladed dagger. 'Anything else in there?'

Thackeray smiled as he bent in the darkness. Cribb's question graphically reminded him of a badly-brought-up nephew at the bran-tub. He groped and came up with one of his own boots and a leather valise. It was thick with documents.

There was one other object at the bottom of the cavity apart from his second boot. A cross-cut saw. Cribb was too engrossed in the papers to take it from him.

'Hadn't we better get after Jago now, Sergeant?'

'Jago? Oh yes.'

Cribb had seen all that he needed of the documents. They were deposited with the other finds back in the broken seat-cavity, ready to be picked up later as court exhibits.

A setback awaited them at the stables. No horses.

'There must be a paddock,' decided Cribb. 'Find yourself a saddle, Constable.'

Thackeray selected the best-upholstered one he could from a selection hanging on the stable-wall and stumbled inexpertly after the sergeant, who already had a saddle slung across his shoulder. They followed hoof-tracks to a small, fenced clearing. Two grey stallions under a tree regarded their approach indifferently, their tails flicking at flies.

'Ever saddled a horse, Thackeray?' Cribb asked, as they let themselves through the gate.

'If I'm honest, no, Sarge.'

'Nor have I. Always a first time, eh?'

'Undoubtedly.'

'I'll take the brute on the right then.'

'Very good, Sergeant.'

'They don't look so friendly now we're near, do they? I'd go so far as to say that mine looks positively vicious.'

'Shall we saddle one between us, Sarge? Take them one at a time?'

'Capital suggestion. Whoa, there! Nasty animal. Better try the other one. I think if you could hold its head ...'

Ten minutes later the horses, still unsaddled, watched the Law retreat, limping and defeated.

'These fights never start on time,' Cribb was saying. 'I've no doubt we'll be there before it's got very far.'

The noon sun bore down heavily as they made their way across the fields towards Rainham. The blister on Thackeray's right foot was now troubling him more than the hoof-kick on his shin. It was going to take at least an hour to reach the station. Then they had to get to London Bridge, find out where exactly the fight was to be staged, and take the first available train there. Jago could be beyond help by then.

'What's that?'

Ahead of them a flock of birds had taken flight simultaneously, plainly disturbed by something. Cribb took out his field-glasses.

'Curious. Take a look. Moving along the line of the hedgerow. If I didn't know better I'd say it was a bobby's helmet.'

Thackeray looked. 'But it *is*, Sarge! It'll be the Rainham man on his tricycle. He's coming along the lanes. We can intercept him by the gate there!'

Both men forgot their soreness and sprinted for the lane. The helmet, uncannily smooth in its progression, threatened to glide past altogether. They shouted as they ran, and the constable came to an emergency stop some fifteen yards past the gate.

'What, what, what?' he said, still seated aloft on his Harrington Desideratum with fifty-inch solid india-rubber-tyred wheels.

'Criminal Investigation,' panted Cribb. 'Sergeant Cribb and Constable Thackeray, investigating a series of murders. We need your machine.'

'Murders? Machine?' repeated the bewildered tricyclist.

'Hurry man! We've got to get to London.'

'Wait a minute,' said the constable. 'Don't I –'

'If you don't dismount at once, sir, I shall be forced to knock you off your machine!'

The constable still looked extremely sceptical, but there was a note of determination in Cribb's voice anyone would have heeded. He clambered down.

'I feel sure that I've seen you –'

'Your bicycling stockings, if you please,' intervened Cribb.

'What? Good Lord! Not my stockings!'

'Help him, Thackeray! Get them on yourself.'

Before another minute had passed the constable of Rainham was seated barefoot on the verge, and Thackeray had taken his place in the saddle.

'Sorry to leave you like this,' explained Cribb. 'Events demand it. If you walk up to Radstock Hall you'll find Mrs Vibart's body in her room. She's been stabbed. We're on our way to make the arrest. We'll leave your velocipede at the station.' He stepped up on to the back axle of the Desideratum and gripped his assistant's shoulders. 'Pedal away, Thackeray!'

Fifteen

The first intimation of anything exceptional that afternoon in Groombridge was a sound carried on the wind, too faint even to be noticeable when there was a flurry of dry leaves along the street. But it persisted, and was heard increasingly clearly, allusive as the resonance in a seashell. Tricks of acoustics in the uneven landscape produced a confusion of sounds supplanting each other from moment to moment: the unmistakable grate of carriage wheels; snatches of music-hall choruses; clattering hooves; unexpectedly clear conversations.

Most of the inhabitants were in the High Street peering towards Tunbridge Wells before the first vehicle appeared. A cart, with men walking beside it. Disappointingly commonplace. But next to turn the distant bend and come fully into view was a gleaming park phaeton with several passengers, and riders in attendance. It was the leader of an extraordinary parade of London life several hundred yards in length that gradually emerged from among the trees lining the road. Broughams and hansoms trundled in formation towards the village as though it were the cabstand in Pall Mall. Members of the gigmanity drove among them, their silk hats flashing intermittently as they passed under the avenue of beeches. Alongside rode numerous horsemen, and a few bicyclists endeavouring to maintain balance and conversation. Most impressive of all, choking the road as far back as one could see, trooped up to a thousand men of the labouring class. A number of others, practised from street urchin days, adhered to the sides of the larger carriages. The huge majority relied on chorusing and good-natured swearing to relieve their footslog. More formidably, sections towards the front carried cudgels ripped from trees along the route. In the thick of them rode the gentry, serene and unperturbed as travellers on a medieval pilgrimage.

Only a handful of spectators retreated indoors. The rest were held by curiosity. More than a thousand marching Londoners from every social class, costers almost shoulder to shoulder with stockbrokers: what momentous cause could possibly have united them? The answer was supplied (to those observant enough to see it) by the wagon at the head of the parade. Besides some dozen unpaying passengers it contained coils of rope, six-foot stakes, mallets and several wooden buckets. Anyone old enough to have heard of a set-to with the raw 'uns knew the impedimenta and could recognize the cart that led the patrons to a 'safe locality', within reach of several county boundaries, where interfering magistrates could not hound them for long.

Three men rode in the grey phaeton. One was obviously to be the protagonist, from the attention he was receiving. A persistent struggling throng moved with the carriage, straining to touch him, his clothes, or just the coachwork, as though contact bestowed some association with his power. For he was a huge man, a Negro, and there was talk that he had never been beaten. For his part, he reclined awkwardly among the cushions, plainly hating the enforced inactivity and ignoring the rapture around him. His two companions in the phaeton compensated by shaking every hand within reach.

The racket of shouting and chanting should have struck panic into Groombridge, without the appalling appearance of the roughs in such numbers. In parts of the home counties prize-fighting mobs were ingrained in popular folk-lore with plagues and witches. Old men told tales of huge groups of roughs and bloods looting and ravaging whole villages unfortunate enough to lie in their route. Strangely, though, the damage resulting from the present invasion was negligible. Two or three windows were idly shattered and one hysterical terrier retired limping. There were plenty of threats with an unbroken flow of East End invective, but even the brandishing of the roughs' 'twigs' had little conviction. For if they looked like a regiment in disarray, in reality an inner discipline governed their conduct. Every one of them saw the need to keep on the move towards the secret venue. Even the necessary taking of drinks at the Lion was a snatch and gulp performance. The return would be different. Shutters would be closed and doors bolted then.

The Negro's adversary rode several carriages behind in a closed brougham with two others, presumably his second and bottle-holder. He, too, had his supporters clustering about the cab, but their behaviour was more inquisitive than enthusiastic, possibly because it was difficult to see him. If it really were he facing forward – and nobody seemed to know him for certain – he looked disturbingly jaundiced.

'No right to be on the box at all, that man,' ejaculated Cribb. 'If a cabby can't cross from Fenchurch Street to London Bridge inside ten minutes he shouldn't have a licence. Now, where's the constable on duty?'

Thackeray spotted a helmet near the timetable-board and inwardly implored its wearer to be competent. He could not remember Cribb in a more peppery state.

'You! How long've you been on duty?'

The young officer looked at Cribb, torn for a moment between an indignant 'Who d'you think you're talking to?' and 'Too bloody long for my liking, mate.' The warning flash in Thackeray's eyes saved him.

'Since eight this morning. Can I 'elp you, guvnor?'

'Cribb. C.I.D.' The constable stiffened. 'A strong party of the Fancy came through this morning. You saw them?'

He recalled them well enough, a rowdy contingent, probably

bound for a race-meeting, he had decided. 'Why, yes, about twelve-thirty, er –'

'Sergeant,' Cribb informed him. 'Which platform?'

'Two, I think –'

'Think? Thinking ain't good enough for me, Constable! Which train?'

Providence had placed the timetable nearby. 'Must 'ave been the twelve-forty-eight, Sergeant. Sydenham, Croydon and Reigate Junction.'

'Next one out's the two-eighteen,' added Thackeray.

In ten minutes they sat in a crowded third-class carriage watching the house-tops of Bermondsey and New Cross pass by the window. Afternoon sunshine filtered through the grimy glass on to the nodding faces opposite, a fat, flushed woman in dolman jacket and a hat supporting a small stuffed bird and satin cherries that rocked with the train; and her two pale sons clutching and systematically emptying bags of jujubes. In the corner a wide-awake hat had tilted forward to muffle its owner's snores. Thackeray screwed up his handkerchief in his pocket and thought about Henry Jago.

'If he's innocent,' said Cribb, unprompted, '– and that's what you'll have assumed, being the generous-hearted cove you are – then you must give me someone else to arrest.'

Thackeray nodded. Cribb's favourite game: find me a murderer and I'll show you how wrong you can be. At least it would provide distraction.

'I'll try, Sarge.' Thackeray spoke at first with his hand guarding his mouth. When the other passengers displayed no interest at all it slipped slowly down to his lap. 'It seems to me that there are three possible suspects from what we know, and that's mainly from Jago's letters.'

'Which could be nothing but ... Never mind,' said Cribb. 'Continue.'

'Well, there's Morgan – the black, D'Estin and Vibart. They all had motives of a kind. The Ebony unquestionably hated being in her power – you remarked on that yourself that night when you watched her massaging him. I find myself wondering

154

whether she had something over him and was blackmailing him. Not for money directly, but for the service he offered – as a fighter, I mean.'

'Quite so,' assented Cribb.

'Now, D'Estin, to my thinking, had an altogether different motive. From what Jago told us of his manner towards Mrs Vibart – remembering that he was only a trainer – I don't think it can be doubted that he was – how can I put it – on more than friendly terms with the lady.'

Cribb raised an eyebrow. 'Plausible, Constable, plausible.'

'They had adjoining rooms when Jago moved in, Sarge. Then there was that argument and D'Estin had to move his things to another part of the house. Now that suggests a lover spurned to me.'

'Crime of passion,' said Cribb.

'Exactly!'

'And Vibart?'

'Ah, yes. Vibart. Now he never seemed to hold his sister-in-law in much regard, and from his point of view I can understand why. When his brother died she became the owner of Radstock Hall and all the estate. Edmund got nothing out of it, and wouldn't until she died.'

'Motive: inheritance,' said Cribb. He glanced out at one of the Croydon halts. 'Those are your three, then. Which one?'

'Well, I think we can discount the Ebony.'

'Why should that be?'

Thackeray looked at Cribb in disappointment. Wasn't it obvious? 'From Jago's account of it he was quitting Radstock Hall. He's been living in the East End for a week, hasn't he? I don't see how he could have broken training to go back to Essex and murder Mrs Vibart, Sarge. Besides, there wasn't any signs of a break-in. We checked the doors and windows.'

'Very well. Go on. Now you're down to passion and inheritance.'

'And there I stop, I'm afraid,' admitted Thackeray. 'Oh, I could construct theories from here to Reigate Junction if you like, but I don't see myself reaching any strong conclusion. One of 'em did it, and wants to implicate Jago by planting the money in his bed, but I couldn't say who.'

'Capital deductions,' remarked Cribb. 'I'd say you've got the answer there unless ...' He stopped and regarded the unlit oil-lamp swinging above them.

'Unless, Sarge?'

'Unless we accept the obvious.'

Thackeray looked away. Like Cribb, he preferred not to discuss the obvious.

However freely Jago's eyes moved about the sights around him – the crowd wedged ten or twelve deep, carriages drawn up behind as makeshift grandstands, a spinney of chestnuts screening the sun and forming two sides of a natural arena – they were drawn back to the Ebony's hands. For the first time he appreciated their size, the breadth of their span, the beamlike thickness of the wrists supporting them and, most pertinent, the shape of the bone-structure. As a youth he had been taken round the College of Surgeons by a doctor-uncle, and a plaster-cast of one of Tom King's arms had been pointed out. The memory of its extraordinary size remained clearly with him. Certainly the Ebony's forearm development was less pronounced, but the fists themselves were arguably more formidable. There was little more on them than skin and bone from wrist to fingertips. Such was the prominence of the skeletal structure that even while the hands rested lightly over the knees the knuckles were deeply crenellated, as vicious a natural characteristic as the pointing of a shark's teeth. In more than a dozen meal-times at Radstock Hall, when the Ebony had sat opposite him, Jago had not noticed the size or singular formation of those hands. All his anxieties until this moment had been centred on his adversary's superior weight and height.

The preliminaries had been got over mercifully fast once the field had been located, stakes set up and the crowd settled – with some encouragement from the cudgel-bearers. D'Estin had looked after the ritual of throwing in the hat to make the chal-

156

lenge and tossing for choice of corner, and Vibart had nominated their umpire. Then Beckett, who was acting as the Ebony's second, had selected the second umpire, and a neutral referee was agreed upon. The right of the second to inspect the opponent's drawers for improper substances was a rule seldom enforced, but Beckett crossed the ring on that pretext to remind Jago of his obligation to stay conscious for twenty-six rounds. The referee made the announcement – almost anti-climax when Jago failed at first to respond to the name of Quinton – and then sent the two fighters back to their corners. The next call to the centre would be the summons to scratch.

Like a dying man, Jago found his thoughts in the last seconds racing over the incidents from his past. Just a few weeks before, these men, Beckett and Foster, who supported the Ebony against him, had existed only as names on the files he kept at Scotland Yard. Now, like the playing-cards in 'Alice', they had sprung offensively alive, and by a strange reversal the people who mattered in his life were distorted in his memory or all but obliterated. Lydia's face became Isabel's whenever he tried to think of it; Thackeray, like the Cheshire Cat, appeared occasionally grinning, with parts of him liable to vanish; Cribb communicated only in riddles. There was no need to pinch himself. Soon enough the attention of those monstrous knuckles would tell him whether he was dreaming.

Where was Cribb?

'Seconds leave the ring, please. Are you ready? Time!'

'What station's this, porter?'

'Tonbridge, mate. You getting out? I can't 'old the train for you, you know.'

In answer, Cribb closed the window.

'Tonbridge, Sarge?' echoed Thackeray. 'That ain't Tunbridge Wells, is it? The stationmaster at Reigate definitely thought the roughs was making for Tunbridge Wells.'

'He'd better be right. That's Kent. My information was Surrey.'

'In that case they ought to have got out at Reigate Junction, Sarge, and the stationmaster would have seen them. He positively said he hadn't.'

'When it comes to prize-fighting, Constable, there's a devil of a lot of queer-sightedness among members of the public. I hope your stationmaster was right. Best we can do is stay aboard till Tunbridge Wells. Good thing Jago's game and can look after himself.'

First blood in the fourth, they had said. Well, they were wrong. The blood did not matter particularly. One expected it, even if it had come a little early and from the wrong source. What bothered Jago was the pressure on his neck, held firmly 'in Chancery' in the crook of the Ebony's right arm. He did not, of course, pretend to himself that repeated uppercuts to his nose – which he was helpless at present to defend – were in any way encouraging. But they were at least delivered with some recognition that the fight was scheduled to last another twenty-four rounds. Their tendency was to flatten rather than fracture. No, it was the simultaneous flexing of the bicep against his neck that disconcerted Jago. Each time it happened, his vision was affected, so that instead of seeing one enormous set of knuckles approaching, he saw two. He could not be sure until contact was made which was the real one.

What the devil! A punch jabbed deep into the tender area below his right eye, stretching the flesh across the rim of bone like a drumskin. Such was the pain that the splitting of skin actually came as relief. He blinked, and his eyelids dipped into the freshly made cut to spread a film of blood across the eye. This was calamitous! Never mind double vision – another blow like that could blind him altogether. Mercifully the Ebony must have appreciated the gravity of the injury. He most decently relaxed his hold, crashed both fists on to the back of Jago's neck, dropped him like a log and so ended the round.

He lay face to the earth for perhaps four thankful seconds before half a bucket of cold water on the back of his head shocked him into full consciousness. A searing pain in the region of his scalp was soon accounted for; someone had grabbed a handful of his hair to jerk his face upwards for inspection. Vibart, talking to D'Estin across his back.

'Nothing too serious. We can move him.'

So he was moved, half dragged by the legs across the turf to the corner. Depressingly undignified, he vaguely registered. Then, as he slumped on Vibart's knee, more water, a dripping sponge that came to his face yellow, but moved away alarmingly crimson. D'Estin, clearly visible now, addressed him: 'Keep cool-headed, Jago. Use the length of your arm to hold him off. We agreed no Suit in Chancery, but if he's tried it once, he'll do it again. Let me see the cut. Lint, Vibart. Not so bad, you see. Hardly an inch long. I don't like this mouse over the other eye, though. That'll split next time he touches it. We'd better puncture it. Where's the lancet, Vibart?'

'Have a nip of brandy and water,' suggested Vibart as he handed D'Estin the instrument. 'There's twenty-four bloody rounds to go, you know.'

'Are you seriously proposing that I should raise a party of men at half past two on a Saturday afternoon? This is Tunbridge Wells, Sergeant, not Scotland Yard. Three-quarters of my men are off duty, and that leaves four of us. I refuse to close the office to hare off after a bunch of London riff-raff that might be over the county boundary by now. I've got the town to look after.'

He *had* to be an inspector. Anyone of lesser rank would have jumped to accommodate Sergeant Cribb.

'You could call them back on emergency duty, sir, if you'll pardon me suggesting it.'

'Emergency?' From the Inspector's tone it was clear that the term was inappropriate to anything that happened in Tunbridge Wells. He was a huge man wedged behind a ridiculously small desk. Getting in there must have been a considerable feat of human engineering, certainly not to be performed more than once a day. 'Listen to me, Sergeant – if you can stand still a moment. I happen to know where three of my best constables are this afternoon, and that is on the cricket-field. The annual match against the men of Maidstone is taking place not ten minutes away from here, and it happens that two of my constables open the bowling for the town and the third keeps wicket. It would have to be a very grave emergency indeed for me to interrupt that. Damn it man, you're asking me to destroy an entire career devoted to cultivating local goodwill.'

This was enough for Cribb. 'I suggest to you, sir, that you reconsider that point. I'm from Scotland Yard, as I told you, and I wouldn't come asking you for support if it wasn't more important than a Saturday cricket match. There are men among this bunch of riff-raff, as you call 'em, who are under suspicion of several murders. If we don't get out there with a group of able constables in the next half-hour there's going to be ugly questions asked when I get back to London.'

'I hope you're not trying to intimidate me, Sergeant.'

'Not at all, sir. Simply stating facts. And this gentleman here,' Cribb jerked his thumb at Thackeray, 'will no doubt have a clear record of our conversation, seeing that he's been specially assigned to accompany me and make a full report to the Director of Criminal Investigation on the conduct of this inquiry.'

Thackeray felt for his pencil.

The Inspector moved.

'A better round, that,' said Vibart. 'Some of this blood on your arms belongs to him, I think.'

'You leave the talking to me,' snapped D'Estin. 'And watch what they're doing in the other corner. If they're using resin we'll appeal to the referee. Now listen to me, Jago. You're just a chopping-block at the moment, and the crowd's getting restless. You've got to come back at him. Use your legs. You should be nippier on your feet than he is. Go for the throat. Good, straight punches with the knuckles pointed forward. Remember what the bastard did to Isabel.'

'Time!' called the referee.

Jago toppled to scratch where the Ebony waited to commence round seven.

*

Sergeant Cribb sat in the semi-darkness of the Tunbridge Wells police van with Thackeray and the three young men in cricket flannels. It was being driven at high speed along the road to Groombridge. Conversation at that level of vibration was difficult, but instructions had to be given.

'The driver should take us as close as possible – up to the ropes if he can. Then it's the men in the ring I want, and the attendants. Never mind the rest. Bundle them in here as soon as you've got the bracelets on 'em. Then we're driving back to Tunbridge Wells. And Thackeray –'

'Yes, Sarge?'

'I want nothing said about us being at Radstock Hall this morning, or what we found there.'

Thackeray nodded sullenly. Cribb might have spared him that small humiliation in front of the local constables. The sergeant was singularly uneasy, and he could understand why, but there ought to be some measure of confidence between them by now. Cribb hadn't intimated even vaguely who it was he expected to charge with Mrs Vibart's murder.

'What about Jago, Sarge?'

'Jago? What about him?'

'He'll be there in the ring, Sarge. Do we arrest him?'

'Of course we do! He's prize-fighting, ain't he?'

Barely two-thirds of the way through, and he was so sore about the knuckles that every punch connecting with the Ebony brought more agony than it inflicted. Both fists were grotesquely swollen; they had an independent weight, like iron gloves. But they were flabby as joints of beef, and almost as raw. Their cutting-edge had been blunted in the first quarter of an hour, turned to pulp in the next. And champions endured four hours of this!

The Ebony, for his part, had kept the fight alive by attacking the body, once the face was too lavishly ornamented with cuts and swellings. Two or three times he had allowed Jago to bring him to grass with a wrestler's hold; once, for self-esteem, he tossed Jago heels over head against a side-stake, and the crowd surged forward from the outer ring to see the damage. By good fortune it was minimal, and in the next round Jago had upset the backers by rocking the Ebony against his own corner-post and bringing a trickle of blood from his ear.

Now, though, there was a change in Morgan's tactics. The lethal knuckles, rested by several rounds of obscure grappling, resumed their orthodox pose, taunting the victim in cobra-like darting movements. The urgency directing them was inescapable. Jago waited, Argus-eyed. With eighteen rounds gone, the real fight was just beginning.

'What have you stopped for now, Constable?' barked Cribb from inside the police van. The vehicle was quite stationary; the occupants, dressed as they were, might have been sitting in any pavilion waiting for a shower to pass.

'Crossroads, Sergeant. I don't know whether to go on to Withyham or take the left turn into Ashdown Forest.'

'Look at the tracks, man, the tracks! We're following a thousand or more blasted men and wagons. If you can't see which route they took you'd better come down and give the reins to me.'

The reassuring clatter of hooves began again.

'A thousand!' exclaimed the wicket-keeper sweeping around for support. 'How can we possibly take on a thousand roughs dressed like this?'

Cribb gave him a withering look. 'You should know. Stand right up to 'em – and if you miss a catch you're for it.'

'How's that, sir?' murmured Thackeray.

'Finish him!' screamed the crowd.
'He's going! He's going!'
'Look out! The Blues!'
Jago sagged on the ropes, unable to visualize anything but general areas of light and shade. Mechanically his head continued to dodge and sway. Hands stilled his pawing fists.

'Told you I knew when to intervene,' said the voice of Sergeant Cribb.

Sixteen

Cribb's first order on arrival at Tunbridge Wells Police Station was for the Ebony and Jago, still linked by handcuffs, to be separated and helped away to be cleaned up and examined by a doctor. The others who had been detained, D'Estin and Vibart (the Ebony's attendants having vanished into the crowd), were taken to the Inspector's office for questioning. Cribb took the chair. Its owner had dismissed himself for a rest after the earlier excitement.

'Now, Mr D'Estin. You say you want to tell me something important. Damned if I could hear anything in that confounded van with the two fist-fighters groaning every time we went over a bump.'

'It's of the greatest importance, Sergeant. I want to report a murder.'

'Murder? What do you mean?'

Thackeray, seated between D'Estin and Vibart, remembered the strategy and tried to look as shocked as Cribb.

'It happened in Essex – at Radstock Hall, Rainham – late last night. Mrs Vibart, this man's sister-in-law, was stabbed in her bed. Morgan, the black, is responsible. I was his trainer at Radstock Hall.'

'Really? My information was that he spent the last week in London, taking his breathings with a man named Beckett.'

'Quite true,' confirmed D'Estin. 'He deserted us a week ago.'

'How could he have killed Mrs Vibart last night, then?'

'Ah, he came to Rainham with Beckett and another man to settle the arrangements for the fight. Mrs Vibart left the party early to conclude the business with Beckett – he had brought the battle-money, you see. The course of the fight was pre-arranged and had to be paid for. Beckett soon returned, but Morgan had also quit the room and he was absent for half an hour or more. He said he was intending to collect some personal articles, and when he returned he was carrying a bundle, it was true, but it now occurs to me – and to others, I think – that the bundle could have contained the dagger that killed Mrs Vibart, and some bloodstained clothing as well.'

Thackeray listened with increasing interest. This was new information; he had dismissed the Ebony from all his speculations because he believed he was in London the previous evening.

'Why should he have wanted to kill her?' asked Cribb.

'Theft. Beckett had just paid her five hundred pounds. Morgan openly despised her anyway. He simply went to her room, stabbed her, and took the money. We found her this morning. The safe in the room was open, and empty. It was obvious who had done it.'

'If it was obvious,' said Cribb, 'how did Morgan expect to get away with it?'

D'Estin slowly shook his head. 'He's not as simple-minded as you might think, Sergeant. He reasoned that we were all too implicated in this illegal fist-fighting to inform the police. But he reckoned without the Englishman's inborn sense of integrity. I'm sure that I speak for Vibart here when I say that whatever inconveniences we face over this fist-fighting nonsense we know where our duty lies.'

'If that were true, sir,' commented Cribb, 'you'd have reported all this to the Rainham police first thing this morning. Now, Mr Vibart. You've heard what's been said. Are you prepared to confirm that to the best of your knowledge it is true?'

Vibart, still spotted with Jago's blood, nodded his head. 'It appears to be the only reasonable explanation.'

'Very well,' said Cribb. 'Then, seeing that we're all upright Englishmen, we'd better call Morgan in and put this to him. Will you fetch him, Thackeray?'

The Ebony was brought in, nursing his left fist in his cupped right hand. His eyes, usually eloquent, were hardly visible for swollen flesh. Cribb explained in detail the turn that the inquiry had taken.

'In short, Mr Morgan, you come under pretty strong suspicion.'

'I? Suspicion? You think I killed her? I didn't know she was dead until this moment! Why should I kill her?'

'For the five hundred pounds Beckett handed her,' said Cribb, unaffected.

'You think I would kill for that? Listen to me, Mister, I didn't need money like that. I was getting paid nearly as much by Beckett, and I stood to pick up another three hundred in side-bets. What did I need to kill her for? I was free of her, and all this lot. This man,' he pointed at Vibart, 'helped me to make an arrangement with the London mob. I was finished with Mrs Vibart.'

'Good God!' said D'Estin, open-mouthed.

'What was in the bundle you carried away from Radstock Hall last night?'

'Why, this dressing-gown I'm wearing right now. If you think this is her blood on it, you're wrong. It's mine and Jago's.' His protesting voice was at crescendo-pitch.

'So you left the room to collect your dressing-gown,' said Cribb calmly. 'Why were you out so long if that was all you were doing?'

'You weren't there,' blazed the Ebony. 'You couldn't possibly know how they were treating me. I stayed out because I wasn't going back to be insulted by men like these two. They weren't my masters, and I could do what I liked. So I stayed in the changing-room until it was time to leave. You couldn't know the atmosphere at Radstock Hall. It was evil. I was glad to get away, I can tell you.'

'What do you mean by that?'

'Things I heard from time to time. It made me feel my own life was in danger there. I wasn't the first pug at Radstock Hall, you know. There were others before me. But they died or vanished. No one would say where they'd gone, but they hadn't succeeded as fist-fighters. I don't know who they were, novices like Jago or experienced fighters like me. Mrs Vibart didn't like to be reminded of them, I can tell you. You know what I think? I think they were put in the ring with hard fighting men and beaten senseless. Mrs Vibart made her money out of failures. She backed other fighters to destroy her own men. That's what she was doing with this man Jago. I tried to warn him to get away – you can ask him if I didn't. I was gentle with him today, though. He'll be quite well in a fortnight. You see if he isn't.'

'Thank you,' said Cribb. 'I shall have some more business with you later, Mr Morgan, but that's enough about this matter. I'll be obliged if you'll leave us now.'

The Ebony was quick to co-operate. When he was gone, Cribb regarded the others with eyebrows quizzically raised. 'Convinced me,' he said. 'How about you, Thackeray?'

'I'm inclined to believe him myself, Sergeant.'

'The timing makes nonsense of it, anyway,' said Cribb. 'Morgan had half an hour – let's give him three-quarters – in which to kill her. But in that time Mrs Vibart is supposed to have concluded her business with Beckett – fifteen minutes would you say? – gone to her room, undressed, washed, folded all her clothes, brushed out her hair, got into bed and been murdered. Anyone who believes that knows nothing about women.'

D'Estin was about to speak, but Cribb checked him with a raised hand.

'Before you say another word, sir, I think I'd better give you all some information. Wouldn't want you to commit yourself to anything before you know why we're here, so to speak. These other men Morgan spoke of – pugilists who trained at Radstock Hall and later disappeared. I'm in charge of an inquiry into the manner of their disappearance. We fished one of 'em out of the Thames, you see. Man named Quinton. No head. You remember him don't you?'

Vibart spoke: 'Yes, he was with us. I didn't know he had an accident though, poor bastard.'

'Didn't you know? He left you voluntarily?'

'Oh he may have had a few wry words with my sister-in-law. He wasn't much bloody use as a fighter, you see. My recollection is that he left after some kind of misunderstanding.'

'He didn't get along with Mrs Vibart?'

'Few of 'em did. It doesn't come easily to a man to be ordered about by a woman who knows a devil of a lot more about the prize-ring than he does.'

'You weren't the expert on knuckle-fighting at Radstock Hall then?' queried Cribb.

'Me? I'm a blasted church organist. I did what I could for her after my brother died. She couldn't negotiate direct with flash characters like Beckett. But she was the authority, not me. You can ask D'Estin here, or Jago.'

'Jago!' repeated D'Estin, suddenly inspired. 'Henry Jago! He's the man you want, Sergeant! He's the only person who could have killed Isabel.'

'What do you mean?'

'It's abundantly obvious when you think about it! He was the only one with a room near hers. Just along the corridor, it was. I caught him prowling near her door only the other night, when he knocked against a suit of armour. He was quite spoony about her. You could see it, couldn't you, Vibart? She didn't care a fig for him, of course, or she wouldn't have matched him with Morgan. When he finally got into her room she rejected him outright, so he killed her.'

'That's all very plausible,' admitted Cribb, 'except for the money. Whoever killed her emptied the safe as well.'

'Then he took the money to make it look like theft,' said D'Estin. 'If you search him he's probably got it now.'

'I went through his clothes myself on the way back in the police van,' said Cribb. 'Unless he had the notes tucked away in the boxing-drawers he was wearing he hadn't got the money. Where is it, then?'

'Must be still in the bloody house somewhere,' suggested Vibart.

Thackeray had listened in wrapt attention. Nothing had been said against Jago that could not be accounted for – well, nothing of substance. The rest was based on supposition. Didn't Henry look a bit dewy-eyed in repose anyway? Yet these men seemed so sure ... And there was still that worrying discovery in his room at Radstock Hall.

'We'd better give him the same chance Morgan had to explain

himself,' said Cribb. 'See if he's able to come in, will you Thackeray?'

There was not much of Jago's face visible when he entered. Someone had been busy with lint and bandages.

'Are you able to answer a few questions?' Cribb asked with a touch of compassion.

The reply was muffled. 'I'll try, Sergeant.'

'I just want you to tell us your reason for prowling about Radstock Hall at night. You can speak freely.'

Jago paused, adjusting his thoughts. Anything that happened before the fight must have seemed like prehistory. 'I was looking for evidence, Sergeant. I did not find it, or I should have reported back to Scotland Yard at once.'

'Scotland Yard?' echoed D'Estin, unable to comprehend.

'Jago is a police constable,' said Cribb. 'One of your good old-fashioned crushers. No use accusing him of murder. He was working for me when he walked the corridors at night, not making overtures to Mrs Vibart. So you see, gentlemen, we're down to two suspects.'

Vibart responded at once. 'Not so, Sergeant. You came late to the fight this afternoon, didn't you? It sounds to me as though you didn't see what thousands of others saw. Give us a view of your back, Jago, and then tell Sergeant Cribb about your feelings towards Isabel!'

'What's this?' snapped Cribb, robbed of the initiative.

Jago stood compliantly and slipped off the dressing-gown he was wearing. His body was hideously blotched with bruises, but the mark that riveted Cribb's attention was the scratch in four narrow lines the length of the back. Thackeray paled.

'How did you come by this, Constable?'

'It was done yesterday, Sergeant,' answered Jago.

'Did she do it?'

'Yes.'

'In what circumstances?'

Silence.

'Ain't it perfectly obvious to all of us?' said Vibart. 'It won't be the first time a bobby's put himself on the wrong side of the bloody law. It was a neat deception sending him to Radstock Hall, Cribb, but you should have chosen someone less susceptible to a woman's charms. Poor bloody Jago. You might get him off with manslaughter if you handle it carefully, Sergeant. We're all discreet men.'

'If Jago is accused,' said Cribb with deliberation, 'the charge is murder. I was at Radstock Hall myself this morning. I found this' – he produced the wad of bank-notes from his pocket – 'in Jago's room under his pillow.'

D'Estin gasped audibly.

'As I said all along –' began Vibart unctuously.

'Permit me to finish. If I'd ever harboured doubts about Jago – and I don't say I had – the finding of this dissolved 'em. If a trained constable decides to place himself on the wrong side of the law, to use your expression, do you really suppose he hides the main evidence under his own pillow? And after the crime is discovered does he still go through with a fist-fight and get battered black and blue for no reason at all? No, Mr Vibart, Jago or anyone else cuts away with the money as soon as those dogs are shot and the way out is clear. It's plain enough to me someone put the five hundred in Jago's room as a safeguard.'

'What do you mean?' asked D'Estin.

'Sharp thinking on the part of the murderer. He expected the Ebony to take the blame – you all agreed he was the man. You had your own plans to even the score, I should guess. But suppose something went awry. Putting the worst possible construction on events, suppose someone else got to know about the murder – a servant perhaps – and brought the police to Radstock Hall while you were at the fight. Wasn't it a smart precaution to have a suspect in reserve? Uncommon smart, I say. If nothing happened our murderer could have gone back to Rainham after the fight, picked up the money and none of us would have been any wiser. Confidentially, though, the money wasn't the only evidence I was looking for. There was the knife, you follow, and there had to be bloodstained clothing. To put you fully in the picture, gentlemen, I found 'em in the cavity under the window-seat – dagger, coat, a case of documents and a saw as well –

now, why would anyone want to hide a common saw? So you see, I can't possibly oblige you by arresting either Morgan or Jago. Your theory rested on Morgan carrying the things away with him. And as for Jago, well, he'd have hidden the five hundred with the other things, wouldn't he?' Cribb sighed with a forced air of reluctance. 'Which means there's only two suspects left for me. You, Mr D'Estin, representing unrequited passion, if I may be so bold, and you, Mr Vibart, on the side of personal gain – inheritance, in fact. There's good arguments in favour of either of you, until we look closely at the crime itself. Remind us of the injuries to Mrs Vibart, will you, Thackeray?'

'Five stab-wounds in the chest, left side,' recited Thackeray. 'Distinct bruising on the left shoulder and the left side of the neck towards the front.'

'Thank you. It's obvious enough, ain't it, gentlemen, that the murderer held Mrs Vibart down with his hand on her neck while he stabbed her with the knife in his other hand? We don't need demonstrations, do we? Now I've always admired the way the handicapped overcome their injuries, and you'll all agree that Mr D'Estin here is a notable example. He can put that one finger and thumb of his to a thousand uses, I dare say. But one thing I don't think he could manage is to hold a dagger firm enough to stab a fellow being five times.' Cribb's eyes darted from face to face like a schoolmaster's checking for a flash of comprehension. 'Now before you tell me he could have held the knife in his left hand, just think about it. The right hand – his injured one – is at her throat, the left hand stabbing her. In practical terms, it can't be done, gentlemen. Mr D'Estin ain't my man. What do you say, Mr Vibart?'

He had no chance to say anything. D'Estin sprang from his chair, upending it behind him, and plunged his hand into his jacket pocket. 'You killed her! I'll settle with you, you bloody murderer!'

'You won't, sir,' said Cribb. 'Not without this.' He was holding the revolver D'Estin had expected to produce. 'Took it off you in the struggle when we arrested you, sir. Just as well, too.

Now sit down, will you, while we settle this in a civilized way?'

'Civilized?' repeated D'Estin, as though the word were totally foreign.

'Will you sit down, sir?'

There was a moment's hesitation. Then D'Estin obeyed.

'Now, Mr Vibart. I suggest that you are the only man who could have killed your late sister-in-law.'

D'Estin's display of violence had shaken Vibart, but he was not ready to capitulate. 'You can suggest what you bloody well like, Sergeant. It's proof you'll need in a court of law.'

'There's cast-iron circumstantial evidence,' said Cribb. 'Motive. Opportunity. Once I'd eliminated the others it had to be you. Your dealings with Beckett showed you had no loyalty towards Mrs Vibart. But you deliberately arranged things so that suspicion fell on Morgan.'

Vibart shrugged. 'That's not evidence enough to hang a man.'

'There's the contents of the valise,' Cribb pointed out. 'I haven't examined the papers in detail, but there's a case to answer for the deaths of Quinton and several others –'

D'Estin intervened. 'No, Sergeant. He's right. A smart lawyer could raise enough doubts to confuse a jury. Without stronger evidence you'll have to release him.' He turned to look at Vibart. 'We'll settle things ourselves – we agreed on that, didn't we, Edmund?'

The false air of familiarity carried more menace than the open threat of a moment before. Jago had a sudden recollection of D'Estin's sinister reference to the man once responsible for the accident to his hand.

Vibart paled. 'You don't believe this nonsense, D'Estin? We've always been friends. Things weren't easy. I can make everything up to you –'

D'Estin smiled grimly. 'Indeed you will. Payment in full, I think.' He turned to Cribb. 'Well, we mustn't detain you, Sergeant. You'll want to question Morgan about the prize-fight. Good thing you can bring a charge for that, anyway.'

Saying nothing, Cribb got to his feet.

In desperation, Vibart looked from face to face for a spark of compassion. Cribb's face was impassive, Thackeray's vacant, Jago's hidden by bandages. He panicked.

'Don't leave me, Sergeant. Not with him –'

'I'm rather short of evidence, sir.'

'God in Heaven, man! He means to kill me!'

'Do you reckon so, sir? We'll certainly arrest him if he does,' Cribb assured him breezily. 'Got your hat, Thackeray?'

'No! Wait, Sergeant!' Vibart appealed. 'I can't face him. I'll say whatever you want.'

Cribb turned. 'Full statement, sir? Freely given, of course? We'll start with the first prize-fighter who came to Radstock Hall then . . .'

Cribb sat in his best suit at his usual place in the Ratcatcher, a tankard of Bass East India in front of him. It had been an illuminating day. 'Report to Inspector Jowett, Great Scotland Yard, 11.30 a.m.,' the message left on his desk had said. There wasn't much doubt in his mind about the outcome of this interview. He felt sorry there was no message for Thackeray, though; getting on in years, of course, and not particularly inspired, but surely worth a lift in rank towards the close of a dutiful career.

The wait outside Jowett's office had been unusually prolonged. It was nearly twelve when the Inspector came out with three other people. 'Ah, Sergeant Cribb! Good gracious, I've kept you waiting. Don't look so concerned, though. Merely wanted to thank you for your stout efforts on the Vibart inquiry. You'll be pleased to hear, I know, that I've managed to convince my superiors that a case like that merits promotion for someone. That's why Jago came in this morning. It's *Sergeant* Jago from now on, and well deserved. First-class investigation. Damned good family too.' He turned to the other beaming visitors. 'Miss Boltover, I don't need to introduce Sergeant Cribb, I believe. Miss Boltover told me quite a lot about her part in the inquiry, Sergeant. And this is Colonel Boltover, school associate of mine. We're just off to enjoy a good meal together, and inflict old memories on these young people. Must be away, then. Have a word with my sergeant before you go, will you? I want you to confirm that our count of crimes in your area is accurate.'

... Count of crimes! Cribb looked up from his drink and regarded the engraving on the wall above him '... *302 rats in one hour at the Hare and Billet, Wimbledon, 7th May 1863*'. For some seconds he eyed the bull-terrier, Leamington. Then he emptied his glass and went home.

More About Penguins and Pelicans